Alex & Nory,
Never stop exploring.

ALSO BY AARON DURAN

La Brujeria

*The Post-Modern Astronaut,
or Frankenstein on Mars!*

Dark Anna and the Pirates of Kadath

*Learn more about Aaron's work at
www.geekinthecitycomics.com*

THE FORGOTTEN TYRS
BOOK 1

WELCOME TO GRIZZLYDALE

AARON DURAN

The Forgotten Tyrs – Book 1 – Welcome to Grizzlydale

© Aaron Duran, 2015

All rights reserved.
Originally published in the United States
by Aaron Duran through CreateSpace

ISBN-13: 978-1508796015
ISBN-10: 1508796017

The characters and locations found within are a work of fiction and are solely from the imagination of the author.
Even incidents that bear similarities to actual events and locations are entirely a work of fiction from the author. Any similarity to people, places, or events is purely unintentional and coincidental.

Book Design: Jennifer Alvin
Editors: Jemiah Jefferson, Jennifer Alvin, and Denise Espinoza
Cover Photo Copyright: David Puerto / 123RF Stock Photo

First Edition: Spring 2015

Acknowledgements

Well here we are, my first novel. There are a lot of people I need to thank for helping me make this book happen.

First, to my loving wife Jenn, who has not only been supportive since the very first day we met, but also got me to sit down at a keyboard and write it in the first place. I really don't think I could have made it without her help.

To my family, who never once told me to put away childhood things and keep dreaming. (Although telling me to put the book down and actually get some sleep was a good idea).

To all my friends that inspired me and pushed me to pursue the dream, to say nothing of their constant cheering when I hit a rut.

And finally to my sister Meghann, who never knew, but was always the first person I ever wanted to tell stories to.
Thanks Megs, you're the best audience a brother could have.

PROLOGUE

Tocho kept running. In the distance she heard the person that fired the shot yell something at her. Even if the rushing wind and screeching beast didn't dominate the air around her, she wouldn't understand the person with the gun. She never bothered to learn the white man's language. Why should she? They never bothered to learn hers. It was yet another failing she would correct if they survived this day. Tocho fixed her gaze ahead. The beast on her tail grew closer and closer. She felt her legs burn in pain, as if small flames reached up from the ground itself and seared her flesh. That pain, she was certain, would pale in comparison to the fate that awaited her should the ravenous creature connect with its claws.

Only a few hundred feet to go. Her people called it Tse'nahaha Ledge, and the cliff was reputed to be inhabited by demons and monsters. She did not believe the stories, and understood the mysterious sounds that emanated from the area was merely the wind moving across the homes of local birds that called the cliff home. All her life, she had laughed at tales of spirits and monsters. "Perhaps I should have paid more attention to the elders," she managed to think as she ran at all speed. Still, Tocho hoped what she knew about nature would save her now. Even the most hungry or infected mountain lion would be reluctant to chase its prey over the ledge of a cliff. Tocho knew this, because she'd watch a deer or rabbit leap to its death, only to see the hunter stop, sniff the air, and walk away in defeat.

Tocho, the young woman named for the mountain lion, ran harder to the edge of the cliff.

The person that fired the gun shouted at her as she pushed herself faster and faster. In the distance she thought she heard her friend Honi scream her name. She tried not to think about losing her one true friend among her people. Little else entered her mind as she leapt from the cliff.

The air rushed past her. This would not be the day to join her ancestors. One way or another, the powers that had infected her lands and her people were coming to an end.

The rope around her waist tightened as fast as lightning. The pain was more than she expected as she felt the world start to go dark around her. She dazedly watched the creature that had threatened her people plummet to its doom below.

Tocho closed her eyes. Five hundred feet above the ground, a rope tied to a tree a mere ten feet above her held her small frame. There was still much work to do.

Tocho passed out.

The air was thick with green smoke. Tocho knew she was either dreaming, or dead, because even the slightest wisp of smoke from a fire caused her to cough and her breathing to become tight. The fact that she was doing neither told her this was no natural smoke. Slowly she lifted herself from the ground. Turning her head, she saw shadows of her village, mere outlines of what her home looked like. There was no life, only the smoke. At her feet, small tears in the very ground revealed the source of the smoke. It wasn't smoke at all. There was a life, a presence to the smoke pouring from the fissures. For all sixteen years of life, her father told her she was far too curious for her own good, and that one day her endless questioning would cause her harm. She shrugged at the memory and reached out to the green smoke.

"I wouldn't touch that," a calm voice said from behind Tocho. "It's very likely your spirit would be forever pulled and locked within the Tyr. If any of us are going to survive this, you can't be lost as well."

Tocho turned to face the voice in her dream. It was a boy. Not a white boy, but not like her people either. His dress was nothing like the clothing the settlers wore, even after they learned how to survive the strong winters of her land. His shoes looked flimsy, filled with a pattern that flickered in the unearthly light. His trousers wouldn't keep out any but the gentlest of wind, to say nothing of protecting his legs while riding a horse. Judging by the way he carried himself, this boy had never even placed a hand upon a horse, let alone ridden one. For all his strange looks, there was a sense of peace and calm about him. Despite her recent brush with death, Tocho felt completely at ease with the brown-haired stranger that stood before her.

"You speak my language?" Tocho asked with a hint of doubt.

"No. I don't. To be honest, I don't even know what language

I should be speaking. Or, if we're really speaking at all." The stranger's words formed perfectly within Tocho's mind.

"Then how can we be speaking?"

The stranger interrupted. "Please, we haven't much time." The stranger stopped. Tocho watched him roll his eyes up and slide his right hand over his scalp. His hands were not the hands of a person that worked outside. No one she knew had hands that soft. The stranger continued, "Come with me if you want to live."

Then the stranger shuddered.

"I can't believe I actually said that. The moment is finally here and I fall back on one of the most tired pop culture cliches."

Tocho raised her hands defensively.

"I won't be going anywhere with you."

The stranger smiled. His posture shifted as he looked back at Tocho. "What I mean is, you don't have much time. Unfortunately, it would seem like I have all the time in existence." Tocho's curiosity again got the better of her, and she relaxed as the stranger kept speaking.

"This place you're in, right now, this is on the other side," the stranger paused as he tried to think of any other word to describe the world both he and Tocho now stood in. Giving up, the stranger sighed.

"I really wish we had a better name for this place. It's called a Tyr."

"No," insisted Tocho, "it's my home."

"Not quite. Yes, this is your home, or it will be if you I don't get you the information on closing the Tyr. But to do that, you're going to need to trap the creature. The one that opens the first Tyr."

For the first time, Tocho heard fear in his voice, and it was not comforting. Tocho reached out as she spoke with the stranger. "Please help us", she pleaded, "we're trying to stop all the beasts that are running wild in our lands."

The stranger reached out to touch Tocho's hand. She did not pull away, but simply stared in amazement as his hands passed through hers. The stranger's calm demeanor immediately slipped away as he realized Tocho was going to leave the Tyr as soon as her friends revived her in the physical world.

"No. Not yet. Don't wake her yet"! The stranger tried to lock his gaze upon her, but she already felt herself slipping.

"The change in the animals is just the beginning. Go to the source of the earthquakes. The first fissure. Go to the first Tyr and read this." The stranger handed Tocho a scroll.

"Take it, while you can still maintain this form in the Tyr. Take it, before you wake up!"

Tocho concentrated as hard as she could. The thin strips of cloth with writing and symbols took shape and became solid in her hand. The strange boy continued to speak, the panic easing a little from his face.

"We can't close them all, but if you can stop the beast from fully forming now in your time, we might have a chance of defeating him forever in mine."

Tocho unraveled the scroll the stranger handed her.

She let out a gasp. "This is my handwriting. I've never written these words."

The stranger smiled. "I know; not yet. I'm cheating. But, it's the only way we're going to win." The stranger started to fade from her vision as a sharp pain grew in the pit of her stomach. She was waking up and it was going to hurt. The stranger smiled even more. Tocho stared at him, feeling a strong connection to this oddly dressed boy.

"This cloth will save my people?" she asked.

The stranger's smile faded a bit.

"It will help."

"But not save?"

The stranger lowered his head. "It will help."

The pain grew sharper as the world around her faded into blackness, and the stranger disappeared.

Tocho let out a scream that could be heard for miles, even in the dense woods of her people. Standing above her, both Honi and the white man with the gun looked stunned. "Tocho, you are out of your mind." Honi grinned as he helped her up. "But that was one for the songs. Songs I will proudly sing if we survive these days."

The white man pointed toward the higher mountain, which was the source of the first quakes. Tocho didn't need to understand his language to know what he meant. She looked in her right hand at the scroll given to her by the strange man in her ruined village. Tocho steadied herself. Honi held her shoulder tighter still.

"Come," Honi said, "let's get you back home. You need rest. We can regroup with the others and fight at first light."

Tocho shook her head, then she looked at the white man and nodded. He nodded back to her, then loaded his rifle with more bullets. For the first time, Tocho was grateful for the destructive weapon, although she doubted it or any tool of man would be enough for what they were about to face.

"No, Honi. We must climb." Tocho looked at the scroll in her hand that somehow had lines, words, and pictures drafted in her own hand. "We must climb."

Together the three walked to the volcano.

They were never seen again.

1

LAST DAY OF SCHOOL

In less than forty-five minutes, Eric Del Bosque would cease to be a grade schooler. He glanced up at the clock as it slowly worked its way to three p.m. Outside in the hallways of Gold Hills Elementary School Eric could hear other kids running and talking. Most teachers let their students wander around a bit during the final hour. Keeping kids calm on a Friday afternoon was hard enough. Tack onto that a promise of summer break. Eric knew the power of floats down Hobo River or bike rides past Devil's Corral was a stronger draw than any lesson about colonial America or long division.

Eric's teacher, Mrs. Fontana, was a stickler for rules. She was, as Eric's mom would often say, "old school." Class didn't end until that clock struck three and the bell rang. And even then, that wasn't completely true. Class didn't truly end until Mrs. Fontana set her pointy-rimmed glasses down for the last time, raised her eyes to the class, and gazed long. She reminded Eric of the great generals or conquerors from his favorite fantasy books. These were the true leaders that knew that everything upon which their vision fell was theirs to command and control. Most kids found that pretty intimidating. Eric knew not to cross Mrs. Fontana, but he also knew she was about as fair as they came. No favors. No special students. No trouble students. You did the work. You got the grade. And yet everyone knew she had a soft spot for caramels, which she gladly accepted during the Christmas holiday, her birthday, and Arbor Day, the last for reasons about which no student had ever had the guts to ask.

Still, for all her strong-handed control over her class, even Mrs. Fontana knew she couldn't keep the shuffling and murmuring contained any longer. The class of fifth graders would only be still for so long, as this wasn't just another end of the school year. This was the last year any of them would sit in this building, walk its halls to the library, or to the nurse's station faking a cold because they hadn't finished the report on the first Thanksgiving. In a few short minutes that part of their lives would be over. Even Eric was not immune to the promise of what lay ahead.

Mrs. Fontana set down her glasses. Her students knew it was coming. Like starters at a race, they all sat poised at their desks, waiting for the starting bell. She smiled, and with an approving nod she stood before her class.

"Students, it's been a pleasure teaching you this past year. I've watched you all grow into promising scholars. Show those teachers at Summit View Middle School that we know how to get young minds ready for greater challenges."

Eric grinned. Most of the other students didn't have a clue as to what Mrs. Fontana was talking about. Some even slid back into their chairs as they expected her to assign summer work, even if they weren't going to have a teacher to hand the work to in three months. Really, that wouldn't have surprised Eric either. As his mom said, old school.

Mrs. Fontana made a sound that resembled a chuckle. In a most uncharacteristically flamboyant manner, she bowed and flung her arms towards the classroom door.

"Enjoy your summer!"

The kids didn't miss a beat, and flung their bags over their shoulders. They stampeded from their desks, into the halls, and out into the great adventure that was summer break.

Except Eric, who just sat at his desk.

"Mr. Del Bosque, while I appreciate your dedication to education and my own penchant for time keeping, when I say 'enjoy your summer,' I do indeed mean that for everyone."

Eric let out a sigh far too deep for someone of his age.

"Yes, ma'am, it's just..." His words trailed off. Mrs. Fontana pushed her sturdy chair to the side and reached her hand under her desk. Mumbling some unintelligible words to herself, she popped open the small door on the side of her ancient looking desk.

"Ah, here we are."

In the four years he had attended this school, he never once heard Mrs. Fontana give any inclination that she was, well, human. That's not to say she was mean or cruel. But like so many kids, it came as a massive shock to learn these adults tasked with the job of dispensing knowledge and responsibility were more than creatures that only lived between the hours of eight and three, five days a week. Mrs. Fontana turned to Eric as her small arm reached into the tiny open door in the side of her desk. She grinned at Eric's less than flattering open-mouth gaze.

"I assure you, Mr. Del Bosque, I am not about to crawl back into my special hovel, only to be dusted off come September for a whole new crop of kids."

Eric shook his head. It would seem she was also telepathic.

"Oh, um, I'm sorry, ma'am, I didn't mean to stare."

Mrs. Fontana's grin seemed permanently affixed, which made Eric wonder if she saved all her joy for the end of the year.

"No one ever does. It's fine. Now, where was I. Ah, here we are."

Her hand slowly withdrew from the desk, holding a rather plain glass bottle of Coke.

"The manufacturers stopped using real sugar, you know? I mean, for us in America it's been nothing but corn syrup for years—decades, even."

Eric had no words.

"Up until a few years ago, they still used real sugar in Mexico which is from where I imported this tasty bottle. It's a real shame." She reached into yet another drawer in her desk, this time without the aid of some magical switch for which she alone knew the combination. Mrs. Fontana brought out a ring of keys. With a flurry of motion, she flicked a bottle opener from the key ring and, with a hint of ceremony, popped open the bottle of soda. She didn't take a drink right away. Instead, she held the fizzy bottle under her queerly angled nose, and for a split second, Eric swore he saw more than happiness in her eyes. Catching herself, Mrs. Fontana took a deep drink of the fizzy brown liquid.

"It's never the same without sugar." She set the bottle down on her desk.

"Shame. I have so few left. And once they're gone…"

She paused. The room wasn't cold, but Eric shivered. "Well, then it's all over." With that, Mrs. Fontana rather sloppily shoved aside papers, pencils, books, and a crystal apple with the phrase Educator of the Year—1985 engraved upon it. Then, with an energy Eric had no idea she could muster, Mrs. Fontana seated herself upon her desk, took another drink of her soda, and with genuine care in her voice said, "Talk to me, Eric."

Eric. Not Mr. Del Bosque, but Eric.

Unable to contain himself, Eric felt the words fly from his mouth.

"I've lived in this town for almost three years and I still can count on one hand how many people are my friends." Eric spread his fingers in an attempt to drive the point home even more. "And a couple of them aren't really friends, they're the kids of my parents' friends, well, my mom. I don't think I've ever heard my dad talk about a friend, let alone hang out with one. He's always working." Eric paused, assuming this was the time when an adult, especially a teacher, would say something inspirational or motivating. Something for him to think on and ponder. Adults were always telling kids to ponder something. As if they could actually learn the secrets of the universe whenever an adult said, "Now you think on that, young man." Eric grinned. There really had to be a way to shut off his internal monologue. He paused longer still, looking directly at his teacher. Mrs. Fontana only smiled; if she had something to say, she wasn't going to let it out now. "Okay. So

I finally do make a couple of friends who don't think I'm this nerd because I like to spend most of my free time reading books."

Mrs. Fontana simply nodded. "There are worse hobbies you could have, Eric."

Eric shook a bit in mock annoyance. Sure, he thought, now she has something to say. He continued, realizing that little tidbit was all she was going to give for the moment. "Anyway, I finally make a few friends and then last month my parents tell me we're going to move."

At this, Mrs. Fontana looked slightly concerned.

"Oh, I wasn't aware you were leaving. We're sorry to hear that."

Eric tilted his head a bit. "We?"

Mrs. Fontana caught herself.

"'I.' I meant 'I.' Whew, give an old lady a few drinks of real sugar and she can't keep her pronouns in order."

Eric shrugged it off.

"Yeah, we're moving, but not out of Grizzlydale, at least not completely.. No, mom and dad found a place up on the hill. Up in Ashen Forest, which doesn't sound all that appealing."

Mrs. Fontana nodded her head. "You do understand, Eric, that Ashen Forest is only a few miles out of town. It's not the end of the world." Eric again, he still couldn't get used to his teacher calling him by his first name. He'd never ever dream of calling her by hers, come to think of it, he didn't even know Mrs. Fontana's first name. If she even had one.

"Mildred."

Eric raised his eyes in shock. Mrs. Fontana continued, "My

first name is Mildred." Mrs. Fontana—Mildred—took one last drink from her glass bottle of Coke and set it on her desk. It hit the weathered surface with a thud. The louder-than-expected impact took Eric out of the moment. He stepped back a bit. There was something odd to this woman that stood before him. Nothing that made him feel unsafe, or even uneasy. But simply something different. How could this possibly be the same person that made his whole class memorize all the state capitals in a week? She grinned even more. "Never fails to amuse me. Students are always shocked when I tell them my first name." She snorted a bit and with a hint of embarrassment, covered her mouth with her hand. "You should see their reaction the first time they see me at the grocery store."

Eric finally summoned the courage to speak.

"Did you know I was wondering about your first name? Before you said it. Did you know?"

Mrs. Fontana's face squished in mock disapproval. "Eric, after all you've learned this year, are you now seriously considering that your teacher—the one that explained gravity, photosynthesis, and long division—is now going to claim that telepathy exists? Not only does it exist, but that I just used it on a boy that's worried about never finding friends in a new home?"

Eric fidgeted a bit where he stood. "Um, no." He let out another deep sigh. "Yes."

She laughed louder than any adult Eric had ever known, even louder than his mom the day she scared his dad so badly he actually leapt three feet straight into the air and clocked his head on the lamp. But instead of being bothered, Eric felt oddly calmed by this all-new view he had of his former teacher. She reached out to him with her left hand, her right wiping away a small stream of tears from her eyes, still squinting a bit from laughter.

"And you would be correct. It does exist. And I am indeed telepathic."

Eric's eyes widened so much he honestly thought they would pop right out of his head and onto the floor. He'd forever be known as the kid that shot his eyes out. Literally. Mrs. Fontana shook her head and looked at Eric. "That's not fair. I'm, sorry Eric. No, I can't read your mind anymore than you could read mine."

Eric jumped in. "Then how did you know I was wondering what your first name was?"

"Well, first off, never end a sentence with a preposition. Ever the teacher. "Secondly," she continued, "I've been teaching for almost as long as your parents have been alive and if there is but one universal constant that all students share, it's the curiosity of knowing their teacher's first name. At least, it is with the teachers that require students to refer to them with a proper title." With that, Mrs. Fontana stood a little taller. "Like yours truly before you."

Eric looked at her with some uncertainty. "Yes, Mrs. Fontana."

She smiled again at him. "You worry too much, Eric. Far too much for a child of your age. You will learn soon enough, the world has plenty to worry about. But it's not for you. Not yet." She walked back over to her desk, opened one of the drawers, and pulled out a book. "Now, this isn't an assignment. I won't check with your new teacher. I won't even ask your parents at the end of the summer. I am placing you on the honor system." She held the book out to him. Although the book looked (and smelled) quite old, Eric could tell it was still in perfect shape. This was a book that Mrs. Fontana took great pains to keep from the harm that came from time and the elements. "I know your parents are going to want you to get outside. To make friends. And these are things that you should do, without question. All I ask is this: During the quiet moments, when the sun has set and you can almost feel the silence in the night air, open this book."

Eric took the book from Mrs. Fontana's hands. He could have sworn he felt a slight shock when she let it go completely. He read the title The Tale of Tocho.

Eric looked up at his teacher. He'd seen that expression before. It was the same look his mom gave him the very first day she dropped him off at school. He didn't fully understand what it meant, but he knew what it looked like. "Who wrote it?" he asked.

Mrs. Fontana sighed. "There's isn't an author listed. It doesn't matter. Just enjoy the book."

Eric nodded. He looked down at the cover, then up at his teacher, and back to the book. "When do you want it back? I mean, I can bring it before school starts in the fall."

Mrs. Fontana slowly shook her head. She placed her hands over his, tightening his grip on the book. "No, Eric, this is a gift from me to you. This is your book now. Until you no longer need it."

Eric corrected her. "You mean finish it."

Mrs. Fontana smiled. "Perhaps." With that, she stood up straight yet again and glanced over her shoulder at the large plain clock on the wall. "I'm sorry, Eric. I seem to have kept you past your bus home. Come on—let's go down to the office and call your mom. Wouldn't want her to worry."

They walked down the halls of the school together. Eric slipped the book into his backpack as they made their way to the office. "Thank you Mrs. Fontana. For everything."

She nodded.

"My pleasure, young man. My pleasure."

Eric's mom picked him up ten minutes later. Mrs. Fontana did not wait.

2
THE NEW HOUSE

Eric's mom, Earlina Del Bosque, didn't even stop to turn around as she set her comically large purse down on the kitchen counter. "I wasn't very happy about picking you up, Eric," she said, finally facing her son. "But, I suppose there are worse concerns for a parent than their child missing the bus because he was lost in conversation with his teacher."

Eric just grinned. That grin got him out of more trouble than even he realized. It was probably something to do with his odd left cheek dimple that seemed to connect all the way to the corner of his mouth. It made it all but impossible to get angry at him. It was like looking at a puppy that just realized it had four feet. Without missing a beat, his mom laughed. "That's not going to work forever, you know."

Eric chuckled. "Sure it will."

As fast as it arrived, his mom's smile faded. Slowly, she planted her hands on the kitchen counter and leaned over. It wasn't enough to make an accusation or be angry. No, this was worse. This was the pose that told Eric that something very serious was about to happen. This was never a good pose. "Your father and I really want you to get outside this summer. Promise me you'll put down your books every once in a while and take in what the world has to offer. Please?"

Eric lowered his head. Although only a few seconds passed, his mind raced with potential answers to his mother's simple and wholly understandable request. Each one would end in her getting angry at him. So, he did what kids had done since the dawn of time. He raised his head, provided the most sincere smile possible, and said exactly what she wanted to hear.

"Yes, mom. I promise."

His mom exhaled. This was a game very well known to them both, and his mom was no fool. For now, Eric's answer would stand. A stalemate had occurred in one of the least dangerous battle of wills between parent and child. His mom knew there were far worse things than a kid that loved to read books and create fantasy worlds in his head. She just wished he would go outside once in a while, and live the adventures he built in his hyperactive brain. Not this time. This time Eric's mom was taking action. She reached into her purse.

"I love you, son. You know that. But I also know that smile. I know what went through that head of yours. So we're going to make a little bargain."

This didn't sound good. His mom wasn't one to use deals or bargains. She was of the "because I'm your mom, that's why" camp, so this was some serious cause for concern. When Eric's mom pulled her hand out of her purse, holding a key.

"Just like in your fantasy books, this key will unlock

treasure. In this case, your books. All of them."

Eric stood in shock. She'd locked up his books? This wasn't fair. No, this wasn't possible. He had so many. Piles of them, enough to fill three cheaply-made cinderblock bookshelves.

"You couldn't have. We haven't even unpacked!"

Although this act of parental tough love was clearly hurting his mom, who really did only want what was best for Eric, she held her ground.

"Your father helped me while you were in school today."

Eric dropped his backpack and ran to his still unpacked bedroom. He swung the door open. It appeared just as he left it this morning: a bed, his pajamas from last night on the floor, everything else still in boxes. Save the four large boxes in the corner clearly labeled ERIC'S BOOKS. Those were open. Worse still, they were empty. All of them.

"Mom!"

His shout carried outside and into the dense surrounding forest, echoing throughout the house that was now his home, His boring and now book free home.

"Now stop, Eric. Sheesh. You'd think I'd grounded you for all summer or something."

"You might as well have. This is stupid!"

"Hey, watch it! Keep up that tone and I will ground you. To your room. All summer. And you still won't have your books."

Eric squinted at his mom. Suddenly the traditional give and take between parent and child didn't seem so funny. He felt something rise up deep in his stomach. Something that just wanted out. His mom tilted her head.

"Use that big brain of yours and think long and hard before

you say whatever is building up in there."

Eric simply let out a big exhale, the pitiful kind that only an eleven-year-old could muster.

Earlina grinned ever so slightly. "Smart." She held the key out again, not so much as a taunt, but as a statement of fact. "Come with me." His mom didn't wait for him to answer. She merely turned on her heel and walked down the hall. Reluctantly, Eric followed. Without even turning her head, she said, "Oh, stop scowling. It's not the end of the world. In fact, I think you can treat this like one of your adventures." Eric didn't think his mom's definition of adventure was the same as his. But he had little choice but to play along.

He opened to the door to his parent's bedroom. It was a place that always felt warm. It was where Eric could go if he had a nightmare, wasn't feeling good, or simply wanted to warm up in the cool morning air. Still, as he grew older, the room took on an air of distance, becoming a place that he would need less and less. It was a strange feeling, one he wasn't ready to dwell on. There were more pressing matters to attend, like what had happened to his books!

Further still into the room they traveled. Though only a few more feet, the tension made Eric feel like he was walking miles through enemy territory. His mom had struck quite the blow against his summer plans. With little pomp and circumstance, his mom opened her closet, revealing a large wooden chest. A large padlock sealed it tight.

"The padlock was your dad's idea. He thought you might try to sneak out one or two. It was my idea to make it look like a treasure chest, though."

Eric tried to look even more annoyed. But, truth be told,

this was pretty dang cool. Even if it did hold all his favorite tales and adventures.

"So," Eric said, "you have all my books in that chest?"

His mom smiled. "Sure do. And your father and I have the only two keys to that lock." She grinned a bit. "I can already tell I've piqued your curiosity. No sense in trying to hide it. I'm your mother; I can sense these things."

It was beyond annoying, but she was right. This did indeed make Eric just a tiny bit curious.

"Here's the deal," she said. "For every day you play outside, for at least four to five hours, your dad or I will open the chest and you can take out a book and read it. You can even keep it in your room." Eric smiled, a plan already forming. "But," she continued, "if you go a day without going outside, and that includes going outside and then just reading, we put one back."

Eric grimaced. There went that idea.

"There went that idea, right?" His mother smiled.

His eyes widened. Her ability to understand his thoughts was more than a little creepy.

His mom went on, rather proud of her plan. "Now, if you play all weekend or, heaven forbid, make friends, we'll let you take three or four out of the chest. But, the rule stands. Stay at home, lose a book."

Eric knew he was beaten. Besides, this did have an air of challenge to it. He would more than rise to the occasion.

"I timed this out. If you stick to the arrangement, you should have all your books back way before you go back to school. We'll even give you some free days to just sit around, outside preferred, and read."

His mom offered her hand.

"Deal?"

Eric tilted his head a bit. She had him, and if he was being honest with himself, he was proud of his mom's cunning use of quest items. She must have been reading his role-playing game books.

"Deal."

Earlina smiled at her son. "Good. Now, go outside. Dinner is at six."

Eric nodded and turned to head outside to greet the forest that would be the setting for his most challenging adventure yet. For a moment he thought about telling his mom about the book his teacher gave him. The book that was sitting comfortably in his backpack in his room. But only for a moment. He had to take his victories where he could. Besides, a little secret now and then was good for everyone. And with that, Eric stepped outside and promptly had the worst afternoon of his young life.

3
THE NEW KID

As backyards went, there was very little for Eric to complain about with his new home. It was true that he didn't spend as much time in nature as a boy his age should, but that didn't mean he couldn't appreciate the potential in an unaltered backyard. This new one was indeed a doozy. Although not quite the wilderness his mom promised, being that he could still see neighbors on all four sides of his house, Ashen Estates Pines wasn't just some cookie-cutter neighborhood for people that thought the town was "getting too big." A concept Eric always found rather odd. While he knew there were smaller towns in even more remote areas of the country, he had a hard time believing the location he called home was the dangerous urban sprawl so many adults seemed to complain. Still, there was something to be said for a location where the homes all looked a little different. Stretching on what passed for a porch, and in reality was little more than temporary steps in place before the real porch went in, Eric looked to his left. It was a simple white house, like something he'd seen in his early nursery rhyme books. Clearly an owner that had little love for the natural look of a pine forest, most of the ground was exposed to the elements. Save a bizarre layer of white pebbles that quite literally covered every square foot of the property, and coming to such a perfect stop at the edge of his backyard that he wondered if someone came out every night with a yardstick and made sure each stone was in its proper place. In fact, the longer he thought about it, the more he started to wonder where the rocks even came from. Looking at his feet, he saw plenty of rocks. Not a single one came in the color of the raw bread dough he saw at that very moment. A question to file away and answer another day. Eric's eyes shifted.

Trucks, cars, and all manner of vehicular movement in various stages of repair blocked most of his vision of another neighbor. What he could make out about this other home filled him with little hope that his mom and whomever this person was would get along. Eric's mom was a bit of a neat freak, and that neatness most certainly extended to her yard. Eric thought it would be interesting to see how well his mom and this neighbor would get along. A dog weaved between the various heaps of rusting metal and stacks of tires. Moments later, Eric saw the reason for the dog's rather speedy movement.

"I've told you a million times, not in the house!" And with that, out ran one of the strangest women Eric had ever seen. She was wearing what some might call pants, but they better resembled a circus tent that was desperately trying to collapse upon itself. Between her varied and far too-vulgar-to-repeat shouts at the dog were shrieks of pain as she ran over all manner of metallic bits. Grinning, Eric saw why. In her haste, the shrieking woman neglected to put on any form of footgear, and each step held the promise of one more shot at tetanus. From her waist up, a massively oversized shirt proclaiming some band he would have to ask his mom about clung to her incredibly small frame. How it stayed on likely had more to do with its mass than any real clinging ability.

The dog rounded what looked like half of a VW Beetle and made a direct charge toward Eric. He simply stood there, still too dumbfounded by the entire spectacle to realize that the dog had no intention of slowing down, at least not until it rammed into Eric at top speed. Who, standing on this rather poor example of stair construction, was all but certain to go flying. In that split second, Eric thought to himself, If I get too hurt to go outside, then my mom can't keep my books from me. A win by way of injury. No, that would be too easy. And, as much as Eric liked the idea of getting all his books back in one fell swoop, even he didn't want to spend the summer in a cast. With that, he braced his body on the front door and prepared to defend himself against the four-legged invader. Eric wished it was only really excited to meet the new kid and not consume him within its enormous mouth.

The hit never came. As the massive dog sprinted toward Eric, he came within a few yards of Eric's neighbor on the right. With speed seen only in cartoons, the dog came a stunning halt, so fast that even the dirt and dust flying in its wake floated past him. In an instant, an animal that was all tongue and slobber was reduced to a submissive creature that couldn't unlock his legs, let alone look up at Eric.

Eric looked around. What the heck had just happened? He

looked at his hands. He wasn't holding anything. He didn't shout. Nothing should have stopped that dog from bounding onto him. His attention drifted toward the house to the right, a nice enough-looking home. Eric actually thought it was the nicest one within his rather limited view. It wasn't a typical home with four corners and a roof. It looked like one of the twenty-sided dice from his role-playing games, with tiny windows placed on most of the flat surfaces. Out front, a pretty covered porch didn't cut and slice into the yard, like so many in the area. This one went around the trees that, no doubt, had stood on this land far longer than anyone else. Benches carved from the very woods sat on the porch. It looked, of all things, like an inviting place. Not a place that would scare the local mutt dead in its tracks.

Except for the barn. Next to the round house sat a barn, clearly on the same property as the inviting home. The barn looked old, but not at all run down. Far from it. Not a single mark or discoloration tainted the dark brown wood. The roof, unlike so many others he'd seen, lacked any signs of physical damage. Impressive for an area that was legendary for its winter snow storms that caused the residents to stay up all night and shovel their roofs. Stranger still was the foundation the barn sat upon. An almost sickly white, the barn stood upon a perfectly smooth slab of what looked like concrete, or maybe even marble. Out of place, but still nothing that would give reason for a charging dog to stop dead in its tracks. His attention was pulled from the barn when his neighbor from across the street finally caught up with both his thoughts and the frightened dog.

"Get your stupid butt over here and leave that boy alone! I

swear, why can't you go missing like all them other mongrels in this place?"

The dog tilted its head up, Eric did the same, and were they able to understand each other, they might have laughed at the shared "huh" expression on their faces.

"I'm sorry about Hoss. He's pretty dang harmless, but sometimes he forgets he weighs about a hundred pounds. Oh, hi, I'm Mrs. Foster, but folks call me Patti. Hi. You must be Earlina's boy. Yeah. I already talked with your mom. Oh shoot, I hope she's your mom. These days, could be step-mom or something. Oh no, now I've gone and offended you. See, this is why I shouldn't..." She snagged Hoss by his rather worn collar. "And you, I swear, you ain't good for nothing but causing me grief. Where was I? Ah, right, so you're Earlina's boy. I hope. Great. Well, welcome to the neighborhood. You come on over soon and meet my girl. She's an okay kid. Heather. She could use a friend ain't horrible. You don't look horrible. Okay, need to run this monster home. Say hi to your mom!"

Eric stood in silence as she walked away. It was only after she was many feet from Eric that he mustered the comprehension to respond to her rambling.

"Huh?"

He watched Patti Foster walk back to the labyrinth of steel and rubber she called home, a now-sullen dog in tow. Eric noticed that the dog took a good long while before turning his gaze from the barn. In fact, it was only when it was no longer physically possible to keep looking did the dog look forward.

"What the heck was all that about?" Eric said aloud. Without thinking, Eric walked down the temporary construction steps and made his way toward the barn that had stopped a charging dog in its tracks. He weaved past tall pines and brightly colored cedar trees. He slowly stretched his hand out and let his fingers dance over the manzanita bushes that towered over his eleven-year-old frame, some of them stretching over him by two or more feet. He'd never had a backyard that felt so very natural, yet strange and alien at the same time. The barn drew closer with each step. His senses, already charged at the idea of just what could be within, were working overtime.

Every bird call and chirp sung out like a chorus, chanting for Eric to move forward to the plain, yet oddly foreboding structure. "You're doing it again, Eric." He, acknowledging his own ever-so active imagination, began filling his head with images of monsters, beasts, or creepy backwoods killers hiding in the barn. As he drew closer, Eric stopped just long enough to stoop over and select a branch of suitable weight and heft. He fumbled for a bit. No mere twig was going to work this time. Whatever his mind was convinced he was going to face, it was going to take more than a quick poke to dog's eyes to do it in.

"Wait," he again said out loud. "What if it doesn't have eyes?" He nodded and snagged what could only be described as a small log. Knocked off one of the larger pine trees in his yard, it had a nice weight. Not too heavy as to impede a full swing, but with proper density to drop a foe should future events require Eric defend himself. He scraped off some of the bark. It was a well-known fact by those that knew the ways of backyard swords that bark, while offering a sturdy grip, was unreliable when the action kicked in. Many an adventurer had been felled by their sturdy bark handle flaking off in the heat of battle. Eric would not fall victim to such dangers. Sure, the stripped wood had less grip, but it was certain and true.

For a brief moment, Eric stopped and stared at his makeshift sword. Deep down he knew it was just a stick. Probably not even a good one, as it fell from the tree, it was likely brittle and was an invitation to get a splinter in the eye. He looked around. Realizing that if anyone was watching, he was going to be known as the weird kid that played Robin Hood in the backyard. He looked at the barn. It was just a barn. His eyes went to his own home. Off-white siding, an off-beige roof, and impossibly so, off-off white accents around the windows. That's what waited for him if he went back inside. He heard a dog yip in the distance. Not Hoss; another dog, no doubt trying to escape its masters. The yip was followed by a cadence of blue birds, calling out in an almost mocking manner. Their cries carried on the wind, as the gentle breeze dusted up dead pine needles at his feet. The sound sent a chill down his spine on a rather warm early summer afternoon. Eric turned his attention back to the barn. His eyes narrowed and his grip tightened. The stick was gone; there was only Pine Bash, his trusty weapon.

"Then again," he proclaimed, and again began his march to the barn.

After a few more feet, Eric found himself at the front door. Be it fate or just dumb luck, the door was unlocked. More than unlocked, it was open, as if taunting him to enter of his own free will. Eric thought back to his books. Entering of one's own free will was never a good start. He shrugged, having come too far to back off now.

Starting to take a step inside, Eric paused for just a

moment, again, mumbling to himself as he often did,

"This might not be the best way to meet my new neighbors, 'Hi, I'm Eric. Don't mind me, I'm just the kid that was breaking into your creepy looking barn because I think it somehow stopped a rampaging dog from ruining my summer that I really am not looking forward to in the first place.'" He looked at the house that shared the land the barn sat upon. A massive "For Sale" sign was planted firmly in the dirt. There was a very good chance that no one lived in the house and that perfectly groomed yard was a result of a dedicated real estate salesperson. "I should just stop talking to myself and look inside." He looked around to make sure no one was watching. "No harm in looking. Plus, I've watched police shows. It's not breaking in if the door is open. Yup."

Eric took a deep breath, and, holding the air in his chest, stepped into the barn. After a few seconds, he slowly let the air out. Nothing. There was nothing in the barn. Sure, a few random tools hanging from the walls, a couple of nails on the floor, and the most innocuous work table he'd ever seen were all that made up the building that promised so much on the outside. Disappointed, Eric pressed further into the rather boring start to his summer adventure. He was going to earn that first trip to the book chest.

For all its banal sameness, there was still something in the air that Eric couldn't quite place. The closest he could compare was the feeling he got whenever he went to visit the school nurse. Not wholly unpleasant, but almost otherworldly in sterility. For a barn that housed tools and other gardening items, the place was clean. The closer he looked, he noticed the barn was unnaturally clean. Perhaps this trip would yield some adventure yet. Upon first entering, Eric wasn't able to see all the way to the end, with the barn lacking any real windows, with only the open door allowing in light. Even under the early summer sky of June, the sun's rays were only able to go so far. In too short a time, Eric found himself in deep shadows.

It was in those shadows that he saw it—a faint green light against the far wall. He stepped deeper still into the barn, clutching his "sword" tighter. His books reminded him all too well of what could be waiting in the glow. So focused was Eric on the gentle green light that he didn't hear the commotion building outside the barn. It grew louder and Eric moved ahead. His eyes slowly adjusted to the dim illumination provided by the glow.

"What the heck is causing this?" He reached out with his pine sword and tapped the source of the light. The wall moved ever so slightly. This wasn't the other end of the barn. The slight movement told Eric this was a door that likely led to a whole other section of the barn. This was getting better and better. Outside, unbeknownst to Eric, whose attention was firmly locked onto the allure of what he could only call a secret door, the sounds grew louder still. And, were he paying attention, he would have heard the unmistakable sounds of bikes coming to a racing stop and multiple voices mumbling about. Although he had no idea, Eric was not alone.

He tapped on the door again. It moved just a bit. It wasn't locked, but also would not freely swing. From within, his intense focus on whatever waited for him behind the door was rewarded with the sounds of movement. There was something behind this door!

Outside, he didn't hear the mass of people gathering at the edge of his yard.

Gathering his courage, he pressed further on the door. What was behind there? His mind raced at what he would find. He had heard stories of buried treasure in Ashen Forest. All the more appropriate that Eric would be the boy to find it. Oh, the stories he'd be able to tell his friends, assuming he made any.

"Who won't want to be friends with the person who conquered the Dread Barn of Ashen Forest?" He again spoke out loud as he pulled on the door. It was stuck. But still from beyond the door, he heard movement. Something was rustling from behind the door. Setting his pine sword down at his feet, he placed both hands firmly on what felt like a rusted handle.

Outside the barn, kids were talking in raised voices. He couldn't hear them and even if he did, he wouldn't have cared. Eric was about to solve a mystery that had no doubt haunted this neighborhood for decades, perhaps even centuries. He would write his own book. With both hands on the door handle, Eric let out a victorious cry as he pulled with all his might on the door. The door flung open, and Eric thought he perhaps put too much into his effort as he went flying back from his own momentum. It didn't matter. He'd done it. Now it was time to see the fruits of his epic labor. Eric stood and was met by the most frightening screech he'd ever heard.

He never got a good look at whatever was behind that door, it was all hair and claws as the creature leapt at him. Eric scrambled for his sword. He tried to defend himself. In his panic, he forgot that he dropped it by the now-open door where this horrible fanged beast now threatened to rend him limb from limb. "Ahh!" Eric abandoned his weapon. Run! That was all he could think. Run for his life. Behind him, he heard the ear-shattering shrieks and cries of a creature that no doubt was meant to spend eternity in the barn, a prison for beasts best left forgotten. A beast he'd let out. Eric would be no hero. Oh no. He would go down in history as the boy that opened Armageddon. Here, in Ashen Forest Estates, the highest neighborhood in Grizzlydale. Eric Del Bosque. Bringer of doom. He ran faster still, tumbling a few times, his knees and palms already raw and red from slamming into the floor. It was getting closer. His only hope was the slightly open door that led outside. He ran harder. Harder and harder still, his rarely stressed lungs screaming from within.

Outside, an assembled mass of neighborhood boys and girls sat on their bikes, each one wondering what kind of chaos was happening in the barn that they all had the smarts to leave alone. Each looked at each other in curious confusion. What the heck was going on inside?

They had their answer milliseconds later as the bruised and slightly bloody new kid came rushing out.

"Nooo!" He screamed as he slammed into a much taller red-haired boy's expensive looking BMX bike. Both went tumbling over each other as Eric did his best to get back up.

"Run. We have to run. I let it out! I let it out!" Confused, the other kids looked back at the barn, likely wondering just who this kid was and what the heck he was screaming about. He was still trying to stand, but only managed to place his knee on the redheaded boy's stomach. The red-haired boy grunted and responded to Eric's panicked actions with a swift smack to his head, but Eric didn't care. He wasn't feeling anything. He only knew he had to escape, had to tell an adult about what he'd done.

"Get off me, freak!" The redheaded boy was much larger and stronger than Eric, strong enough to even toss Eric to the side like a ragdoll.

Eric stopped long enough to warn these kids that clearly had no sense of self preservation.

"You don't understand. We have to..."

He was cut off by a giggle. It came from a girl taller than everyone else in the pack. She had spiky blonde hair and a face filled with reddish freckles that looked a little out of place on her rather tanned skin. The look of a person that probably shouldn't spend as much time in the sun as she did. The giggle grew into laughter as others joined her.

"Why are you laughing? I freed a monster from within. It's going to, to... Oh. Crap."

Eric never finished his sentence. He looked back at the barn and the open door. No longer filled with panic at being disturbed by a nosy kid that should have known better, a fat orange cat sauntered out of the barn towards the round house.

So much for the Beast of Ashen Forest. The laughter drowned out his heavy sigh. Eric glanced at the tall girl, her eyes tearing up from laughter, then looked at the redheaded boy. Eric saw the fist coming, but lacked any energy, and if he was honest, the smarts to back up. With an impact he didn't think was possible, even from a boy that size, Eric felt all the air violently leave his chest and out of his mouth.

"That's for my bike!"

Still not finished, Eric felt a small smack on the back of his head from yet another boy. The head smacker also replied. "And that's for taking our bike trail."

Eric got his breath back and looked around. Two boys, who clearly had anger issues, and a girl. A girl that by her looks just had to be Mrs. Foster's daughter, although she already looked taller than her mother.

"Uh. Uh. Sorry. I. I." The combination of Eric's own imagination-fueled insanity and the very real pain of taking a shot to the gut was more than he could take. Eric fell on his butt and shut down, doing his best not to cry. The kids got back on their bikes and rode off into Ashen Forest Estates.

Only the tall girl bothered to look back at Eric.

In all recorded history of being the new kid, this was, without a doubt, the worst origin story of all time.

4
THE FIRST DINNER IN THE NEW HOME

Eric sat quietly at the dinner table as both his mom and dad drummed on about their work days. Although he usually found such conversations mind-numbingly boring, he was grateful the conversation hadn't yet turned to him and his awkward first day. He reached for the middle of the dinner table to grab another slice of warm garlic bread, and without notice, let out a wince. "Ow, eeesh."

His mom turned her attention from tales of state bureaucracy to her cringing son.

"You okay, mijo?" Her tone suggested she was in a good mood, though not overall excited. Her expression deepened a bit when she saw just how much pain Eric was in. He did his best to cover.

"It's nothing, mom. I think I must have—um, I must have pulled a muscle. Must have."

His dad raised an eyebrow and set down his fork, the meatball attached to the end of it rolling off and onto the table.

"Really, boy, you think we're going to... Shoot," His dad hated losing food, not that a meatball rolling off his plate and onto the table was going to stop him from eating it. Right on cue, his dad plucked the rogue food item from the table and into his mouth. Not waiting to finish chewing, he continued his mild interrogation.

"Got it! As I was saying, do you really expect your mother and I to believe you when you say you pulled a muscle? What? Where you actually outside, doing some heavy lifting?"

His mom, keeping her look of concern at her son, changed her tone a bit.

"Franco, don't be that way. He was playing outside, we started the book game today."

"I still find it hard to believe he pulled any muscles. He's gotta have them to pull them."

His mom finally turned her gaze from Eric to his dad.

"That's enough! You aren't one to make jokes about staying in shape. Why don't you shove another meatball into your face."

These petty arguments happened a lot at the dinner table, generally when both parents lacked anything mundane to talk about. Work stuff? Sure, they could go on and on for hours and not raise a voice. But, the moment it was something to do with Eric, then conversations always turned a little nasty. While it still bothered Eric that most of their fights centered around him, he could at least take a little comfort in knowing they weren't asking about his stomach. As long as they kept focused on each other, he could slip away and clean the dishes. Thoughts that were quickly dismissed as his mom raised her voice, signaling the end of this dinner's entertaining spat.

"Enough! Eric, lift your shirt. I want to see what happened."

Eric looked down at the table, doing his best to be blasé. "It's nothing, mom. Honest, I just got a little excited exploring the area. I just fell ."

"Oh, first you pulled something and now you fell." His mom wasn't buying it. "Nope. I want to see. You know your great-great grandmother died from a pulled groin."

His dad let out a sigh.

"For the love of... Earlina, every time one of us gets a sliver, you have to bring up your great-grandmother."

His mom's voice grew in annoyance. "It's true."

"I know it's true, babe." Babe—that's what his dad always called his mom when he was trying to soothe a potentially tense situation, "But she was also a hundred and five years old. Not to sound cruel, but a heavy wind would do you in when you're a hundred and five years old."

His mom simply glared at her husband. Wisely, Franco Del Bosque turned his attention back to his spaghetti and meatballs, twisting a few noodles with his fork. Without even turning her head back to Eric she demanded, "Shirt. Lift it. Now."

There was no hiding. Eric slowly lifted his shirt up, far higher than his mom needed, but high enough so that he couldn't see her face when the inevitable happened.

"Sweet merciful mother Mary! What happened?" Eric didn't need to look to know his mother had just crossed herself. Even his dad let out a whistle at the sight at what was by now a bruise the size of his dinner plate. Eric didn't lower his shirt.

THE FIRST DINNER IN THE NEW HOME

"Fell." Which, he reasoned, wasn't a total lie. He did indeed fall. After taking a sock to the gut, but he did eventually fall and that was the story he was sticking to. Eric wasn't completely sure his mom was going to buy his half-truth. Her words following an uncomfortably long pause confirmed his suspicions.

"Fell?" She gently placed the tips of her fingers on his bruise. Reflexively, Eric pulled back in a wince of sharp pain. "Where are Earth could you have fallen and caused this? Don't lie to me, Eric; did one of the neighborhood kids…" She paused mid-accusation. "Mijo, pull your shirt back down. I'm not mad."

Eric did as he was told. The eyes of both of his parents were intently fixed on him. Their gaze had an almost tunneling effect on him, as if both were digging deep into his mind to find the truth.

"As I was saying, I'm not mad, Eric. Just concerned. If one of the neighborhood kids did this, I need to know. We can't have bullies shoving people around."

Eric really did love his mom. She was hard on him, no doubt, but if there was ever a case that needed the mythical knight in shining armor, his mom was there. She wasn't a very tall woman; in fact, he figured in a just a year or so he'd be taller than her. But she was fierce. He'd read stories about people in times of great stress finding strength that made all but the largest of athletes pale. His mom was that kind of person. Only she didn't need an emergency. She had some kind of switch and she could flick it on with but a moments notice.

On the other hand, as Eric was slowly learning, there was

a time and place for having your mom swoop in and save the day. He glanced at his father. They weren't the closest they could or even should be, but they also both knew when it was best to band together, when to play it close to the chest and let Earlina know that things were going just fine. With her eyes fully locked on Eric, she didn't notice as his dad gave him a slight nod. Whatever Eric was about to say, as long as he didn't go too crazy, his dad would back his play. It wasn't much, but it was enough, for now.

With that in mind, Eric looked his mom in the eye and stuck to his story. "I was exploring, like you wanted, and I got a little carried away." His dad gave him a look that said to rein it in; too complicated and his mom would see right through the lie. Eric took a deep breath. Although this would guarantee another awkward conversation later in the week, he knew exactly how to get his mom to believe him.

"I was pretending to stalk some monsters and I stopped paying attention. I tripped and fell hard onto a log. Sorry."

His mom looked him over a few more times, her protective visage slowly giving way to a whole different look of concern, worried that her only child would never pull his head from the clouds, far more happy in the world within his mind than the one all around him. She simply nodded and let out a sigh.

"Okay. I just wish you would— Listen, there is so much out there that you're missing when you create these worlds in your head."

Eric was used to this talk. He'd been hearing it more and more lately. Surprisingly, his dad spoke up. The man that understood Eric's hobbies and interests even less came to his defense.

"Earlina, let it go for tonight. We asked him to go outside and get into trouble. Let's not berate the boy for doing exactly what we asked of him." He turned his look back to Eric, not really pausing to take a breath. "But let's try and keep at least one eye in the real world. Okay, buddy?"

"Right, dad."

Eric could tell his mom wanted to talk more about this, but she relented. In a way, his dad was right, even if Eric did feel bad about lying, even a little, to his parents about what really happened. Although he knew he was pushing his luck, he knew there wouldn't be a better time to bring up the chest of books than right now, when neither parent could corner him as to what really happened today. Sheepishly, Eric set down his fork and cleared his throat.

"So, as you both saw, I did play outside today. Which means..."

He didn't even get to finish. His mom exhaled and reached into her pocket. "You really do have a one track mind, don't you, Eric?"

He plastered that grin of his as wide as it would go and snagged the keys from his mom's hand. Forgetting the dull throb of his stomach, he leapt from the dinner table and made a beeline for his parents' room.

"Oh, sure, you're excused from dinner, son," his mom yelled down the hall.

Echoing just a bit, he replied,

"Sorry, can I be excused?"

His dad laughed at something his mom said and judging by the follow up comment from his father, it wasn't something he'd be repeating around Eric. Not for a few years at least.

Holding the key firmly in his right hand, Eric lifted the comically oversized padlock with his left, inserting the key and turning. The lock opened with a satisfying click. Eric chuckled a bit to himself. It was nice to know that his mental image of a large lock opening matched the real thing. If only that were the case with everything his imagination came up with. Shaking his head, he went to open the lid. This was no time to get distracted. The pain in his gut reminded him that he earned this trip into the book chest.

"Where do I start?" Eric asked aloud as he looked within the chest that, just as his mom said, contained every single book he'd ever owned. He'd like to say he'd read every single one in the chest, but that wasn't the case. He didn't understand the concept of hoarding, but he did know how it made him feel to see a wall full of books. As such, there were quite a few he had every intention of getting to, it just hadn't happened yet. The names offered so much promise. Lewis, Tolkien, Butler, Le Guin, Asimov, and so many others that could take him anywhere. He skipped them all as he thought of a more practical book to read.

"I need to learn how to dodge a punch."

He pushed more books aside and there it was, even with its torn cover (as he found it at a garage sale well over a year ago). Jeet Kun Do by Bruce Lee. The Bruce Lee. Yup, if he was going to survive this summer, he was going to learn from the master. Or, at least from whom he'd been told was the master. He'd never actually watched any of his movies, but he'd heard his relatives talk about the actor on more than one occasion. And some videos he'd seen online did look pretty great. Yes, this book would be perfect for him.

"You get to pick one and then close the chest. You can't just sit there and read them. That's cheating!" yelled his mom from the other side of the house. Eric flinched at the abrupt shout. He shut the chest and turned to leave. "You better lock it!" Dang, his mom was good.

"I wonder if Bruce Lee ever had to deal with this kind of treatment," Eric mumbled as he walked back to his parents. His mom was waiting for him in the kitchen, her arm outstretched and hand open waiting for him to deposit the key. He did so without hesitation. His mom smiled a bit when she saw the book tucked under his arm.

"You know, we can sign you up for lessons if you want to learn martial arts. It would probably be very good for you."

He barely slowed down as he raised the book a bit in his hand. "Nah, this will do." His mom was about to counter when Eric again used a tactic that would, sadly, end her attempt at buying him lessons. "Besides, I just need it for reference for my games."

His mom let out a sigh.

"Of course. Never mind."

Honestly, he didn't like saying these little white lies to her. It was just easier than going through what really happened and why he grabbed this book first. He stopped. Something told him he needed to turn around, to tell his mom that he was glad she was there, trying to help. Eric turned to his mom and a look at her face let him know that he was correct. While not hurt, Earlina had the look of a parent that really did want what was best for her child. But she also knew Eric was getting older and some choices had to be his to make. Although Eric didn't understand why, he felt like he needed to thank her. He tucked the book back under his arm and walked back to his mom. He put his arms around her and hugged her, though not too hard; that stomach pain got worse on contact.

"Thanks, mom. And, maybe we can look at places for me to get lessons." He added in his mind, because I think I'm going to need it.

She smiled back and held him a little too tight.

"Monday morning, we'll go into town and find a place." She slowly let him go. "Now go read your book. I can tell it's driving you nuts."

With that, Eric went into his box-filled room and encountered something strange.

There, sitting on the bed, was the book given to him by his teacher. The book he'd sworn he'd kept in his backpack. "Maybe mom found it? No, that doesn't make any sense. She would have just added it with the others. She wouldn't even be sneaky about it. She would have proudly proclaimed her discovery with me, probably over dinner."

Eric stopped himself.

"I'm talking out loud to myself again. It's starting to get annoying and I'm the one talking." Eric shook his head. Now he was arguing with himself. Still, it was quite the mystery. Looking at his bag, it was right where he left it, tucked in the corner. Still zipped shut. Confusion gave way to curiosity as he set his book on Jeet Kun Do down. Bruce Lee would have to wait.

He hopped onto his bed, crossed his legs, and opened The Tale of Tocho...

5
THE TALE OF TOCHO

The ash from the volcano covers so much of the sky now, I don't remember how long it has been since I've seen the sun rise and fall. There are only degrees of darkness. The very trees that I once took such solace in sitting under now betray me. The sickness that burst from the ground now infects all that it touches. But even this green sickness is nothing compared to the beast that stalks these cursed woods.

It seems like a lifetime ago that Honi, the white man from the town (who I learned was called Thomas), and I, started our quest to end the creature. With the strange words written on thin cloth, we tracked the source of the beast to the very mouth of volcano.

I never told my companions the truth about the writing. Thomas didn't give my story a second thought. But Honi—my dear friend—he saw the lies on my face. He knew what I held did not come from our elders. So strong was his fear, his desire to end what was threatening us all, he went along with my lies. Lies that cost him his life.

I will never forget the horror as the beast entered the mind and heart of poor Honi. It grew stronger, no longer needing to hide within the form of animals. We made perfect vessels for its vile powers. The fight was brutal and savage. Thomas was brave. Braver than I ever thought possible of the white man. He stood his ground against poor Honi so that I could read the words. May my ancestors forgive me for I read the words and trapped the beast. I trapped my friend. Forever.

Eric sat the book down and turned back to the inside cover. Again he looked for some kind of marking, something that would tell him the person that wrote this book. Nothing. "Thanks a lot, Mrs. Fontana. This is going to drive me crazy. I don't even know what this Tocho person is going on about." Eric shook his head. At least it was interesting, if a bit confusing. Eric flipped through a few more pages. The story almost seemed to backtrack. Eric was a fan of starting a book off with some action, but it was starting to look like this was all there was to this Tale of Tocho. A few exciting opening chapters, then nothing but a bunch of rambling from whomever this Tocho girl was. Still, Eric was not one to give up on a book—well, that wasn't true. There were some that were truly awful and he proudly set them back, never to pick them up again. However, to give in after only a few pages? No, that was not going to happen.

Turning back to the book, Eric's eyes drifted toward his window. The sun had finally gone down, although not much lower than the horizon of the town proper. Ashen Forests Estates felt a little darker than Grizzlydale, although the town sat a short five miles down the mountain. It was, for lack of a better term, rather peaceful, although he'd be lying if he said that part of his mind wondered just what the forest held once the sun dipped over the horizon for the night. His science class told him that nothing changed, save a few nocturnal creatures that everyone promised were more frightened of humans that he of them. He smiled; tell that to the cat that darn near killed me today. As in response to the memory of that day's events, his stomach sent a faint but still painful reminder.

"How am I even going to survive this summer? Maybe I'll get lucky and the volcano will go off again. Force us back into town." Eric sighed. Sure, he thought, and it will all happen before tomorrow morning. No, there's no avoiding the truth. This is my home now and I better get used to it. He let out a large yawn and turned back to his book. If he kept reading, it meant he wouldn't fall asleep. If he didn't fall asleep, then morning would never come. He shook his head at no one. "Sure, Eric, that's sound logic." He turned back to the book.

I've made it back to a safe spot. The ground still rumbles from time to time. I'm afraid to return to my village, for fear of what I might find. No, this is a safe spot. Although it's hard to track the passing of time, I think it's been a few days since Thomas and Honi both gave their lives in trapping the beast. How am I even going to survive The beast. How can something so horrible and unnatural also seem so familiar? I remember stories told to me as a young child. But those were just stories meant to keep the young in line, symbols to prepare us for adulthood, for when we would be needed to lead our people into the future. There is no way the elders were serious. But here I am, huddled in a small cave, days from my home, hoping the beast of my childhood stories has not returned to finish its horrible task. What happened here can never be forgotten. No one must forget the bravery of my friend and the stranger that joined us.

Eric smiled as he read, wondering what this Tocho would think of him, running like he had in the face of what turned out to be a frightened cat. Eric stopped for a moment.

"Green light?" He pulled his blanket tighter as a slight shiver went down his spine. "I saw a green light. I could have sworn I did. Right before the cat jumped." He paused for a moment as the thought danced around his brain. No. He was imagining things. And besides, this Tale of Tocho was fiction. It had to be; it was, after all, written in English. He was fairly certain her first account story would not be written in the language of the western traveling pioneers that had only arrived a couple years prior. This Tocho had to be a fictional character. With that thought, Eric again wondered what she would think of him. Would she laugh at him, or would she say he was right to run? And with that, Eric knew he was doing what he'd done so many times in the past with stories. He was putting himself in the tale. Finding connections with his own world to fit within the pages. It was a good sign. It meant he was in for a very solid read, so solid that he might be willing to forgo a trip or two to the book chest. This Tale of Tocho was no small book. This was at least four days' worth of reading for him.

His thoughts were broken as a short but no less loud wail caught his attention outside. With a slightly embarrassing yelp, Eric dropped the book and leaned his head over his window to try and get a better look at what made that sound.

Outside was a darkness he'd never really experienced before. Nothing sinister by any stretch of the imagination; no, this was a total and complete darkness. For although Grizzlydale was a small town, it was still a place with a few thousand people that lived relatively close to each other. Not like what you saw in large (or even small) cities, but still close enough that the random house or street light pierced the dark sky. Here, in Ashen Forest Estates, it was something completely different. What few neighborhood houses had porch lights were almost immediately sundered by the dense pine forest. Even the air seemed to carry a weight that hindered the passage of light. And so, looking outside, Eric was shocked that he could still, somehow, see a slight outline of the barn that was the source of so much embarrassment just a few hours earlier. He heard the shriek again. Straining against a window he dare not open, lest whatever was making the sound get in, Eric tried his best to learn the source of the horrible sounds.

"You've got to be kidding me," Eric said a little too loudly as his breath fogged up the window. Even in early summer, the nights in Ashen Forest got just cold enough to mist. Wiping away the small amount of fog on his window, he strained again. The barn. The sounds were coming from the barn. Creepier still was the faint green glow emanating from the small sliver of space between the wooden walls and the stone floor.

"No way, that's just not possible. Whatever was glowing in the room this afternoon can't now fill that entire barn." Another shriek flew into the night sky. Eric jumped back from his window. He took a few more steps back. "Okay, I need to knock it off. Mom is right. I do spend way too much time in my own head." He took a few more steps back, toward his bed and picked up The Tale of Tocho. "And buried in these books." His own voice trailed off as he turned the old book slowly in his hands. It didn't make any sense, but for reasons he couldn't explain, the book felt warm, as if he'd been grasping it for hours. Still holding the book, he turned his attention back out his window and toward the barn. The glow was gone. Standing perfectly still, he listened. Minutes felt like hours, but Eric only heard his own breath slowing entering and leaving his body. Nothing. The shrieking, along with the green glow, was gone. And with it, the book felt cool again. He turned his face down to his hands. "Just a book." Slowly he opened the book again, skipping back from where he stopped, Eric found a passage that he read over and over again.

I have to remember how this all started in case the cycle begins again. Those that come after me must be prepared. They must be ready to put down the beast before it ever gains strength again. It started with the earliest rumbles. The ground shook. It frightened those that didn't understand. But our elders, they who had been around for so many years, knew that the same thing that gave us rich soil and thriving animals also shook the ground at times. They would tell us that our price for such full lives was a visit from mother nature's more chaotic elements. We took it all in stride. It was the way of things, and a small price to pay. Until the day came when the very land opened up. Until the green flames burst from the ground.

Eric set the book back on his bed. He looked outside at the barn yet again.

"Just where the heck did we move to?"

Eric pulled the blankets over his head, only leaving a small sliver for air to come and go.

"And why is my room so close to that dang barn?"

In time, sleep came to Eric. In his dreams, the shrieking continued.

6
OUT AND ABOUT IN ASHEN FOREST ESTATES

"Wow, I didn't think my skin could actually produce every color in the rainbow." Eric leaned in a little closer to the bathroom mirror as he took in his bruise, spreading like a multi-colored amoeba around his belly button. If it didn't hurt so much, Eric would have laughed at how funny it looked. "Beware the belly blob! Thrill as it engulfs the nerdy boy!" Eric didn't care about the pain; he was going to laugh at his own misfortune. Why not? Everyone else did. With that thought, Eric let out a small sigh, "Maybe I shouldn't laugh. I mean, first impressions and all. No matter how hard I try, there is no way I'm going to be able to avoid those kids." With that, Eric lowered his shirt, brushed his teeth and went out to have a big bowl of incredibly bland but healthy cereal. He would, much to his mother's dismay, cover the cereal in sugar before adding the milk.

Right on schedule, his mom watched him prepare the bowl.

"Why do I even bother buying the healthy stuff?" she

asked.

Eric, with a mouth full of toasted oak bran surprise (or whatever it was called) replied, "Das a bery good question mom." He took a big gulp and continued with a clean mouth, "Why do you bother?" It wasn't so much a battle of wits between Eric and Earlina, but more a weekend ritual that had become almost comforting. Like that cartoon with the wolf and sheep dog as they punch their daily timecards. Eric smiled at the idea of his mom constantly having to blow the hair from over her eyes as he snuck around in a sheep costume. Yeah, Saturday morning breakfast was just like that. His mom quickly changed the subject as she poured her second cup of coffee.

"What do you have planned for today?"

Eric moved his spoon around a bit in the bowl, as if the milk and various bits within would provide him with all the answers his mom wanted. It would have been easy to just tell her "stuff and things," but the truth was, Eric was actually looking forward to exploring the neighborhood, and doing his best to avoid the deadly Ginger Fists of Fury he knew all too well. With all that rolling through his head, Eric took another bite, set the spoon back into his bowl, and told his mom what he planned to do.

"I think I'm just going to hop on my bike and wander the neighborhood. See what's around."

His mom looked concerned.

"I'm glad you want to go outside, but I am a little concerned about that bruise." She paused for a moment, a moment that suggested to Eric that he might end up spending the bulk of his first summer vacation weekend on the couch. Which, to be fair, was normally something he'd have no problem with. But his desire to stay in simply couldn't hold a candle to the curiosity that was coming over him. Punching from the local bully notwithstanding, there was just too much going on in his head to ignore. Between the strange sounds and glowing next door, to the memories of this Tocho girl from his book which seemed to explain some of his own encounter, Eric had to get outside. His mom stood even stiller, if that were possible. She took a slow sip of her coffee and he watched as she let it roll around in her mouth. It was kind of weird, but he knew that meant she thinking. That, and her weird habit of noisily sucking air in through her teeth. Parents were strange creatures indeed.

"Okay, but I don't want you going too far. In fact, I want you to stay within shouting range."

Eric smiled a bit, wondering if she knew just how well sound traveled in the woods. He might be just a kid, but unlike his mom, he had spent his whole young life in the country (well, small town; same thing). His mom, however, was a city girl, transplanted to the sticks he called home only a few months after he was born. Staying within shouting distance only meant a block or two to her. But to Eric, that meant some deep travels into the woods were not off the table. Not that he would dare tell his mom that.

"I promise. Shouting distance." With that, Eric slurped the rest of his milk and went back to his room to get dressed for adventure.

Eric stood outside, holding the helmet his mom made him wear firmly in his right arm. It wasn't the coolest looking element in his riding attire, but being cool was something Eric had given up years ago. "And if I'm being honest with myself, wearing this in a whole new landscape isn't the worst of ideas. It's not like I'm worried about making a bad first impression or anything." He made his way to his bike. It wasn't anything special, but like a certain spaceship that could travel at point-five past lightspeed, it had it where it counts. In truth, he rather liked his beat-up beast of a bike. No frills. No fancy brakes or gears. This was a pure BMX-style bike. Sure, it weighed a ton, but Eric was fairly certain he could ride it off a cliff and the bike would fare considerably better than he would. And he was grateful. His wasn't the most well-off family in town and even as a secondhand bike, it did its job incredibly well. "Or at least I think it will," he admitted out loud. Beyond riding to the library and back when they still lived in Grizzlydale proper, his bike really hadn't been put through the paces. "Well, buddy, that's all going to change today. You and me; into lands unknown we go."

His mom chimed in behind him.

"Not too far into lands unknown. Also, stop talking to yourself. It just looks weird."

Eric grimaced. His mom was right; that really was something he had to work on. If only he didn't find his own thoughts and conversations so dang interesting.

"You're doing it again, son."

Eric sighed.

"I'll be back for lunch!"

And with that, Eric donned his helmet and took off down the street. Varied houses to both side; ahead, a slight hill with wonders to discover. Although it wouldn't take long for Eric to have his first real taste of living outside the town of

Grizzlydale. As he stood up to pedal over the small hill, Eric found himself locked into the worst game of chicken of all time as a rather nasty and angry-looking dog started to charge directly at him. Unlike the rather mangy but wholly harmless dog across from his house the day before, this massive animal had one look on its face. Get the fleshy one. Eric slowed for just a moment as he contemplated what his next move should be.

The dog was almost on him when he made his choice. He was too far down the hill to turn around and pedal back. Besides, there was no way he was turning his back to this monster. Screaming would only bring his mom out and just as he didn't want to tell her why his stomach had a bruise, he wasn't ready for her to play savior here just yet either. (Although he was glad she was gifted with first aid, which he felt he was going to need soon enough.) No, instead his panicked gaze looked toward the dense woods to his left. There wasn't any sign of a trail. "Okay bike, time to see just want you can do." With a standing lunge and a huff that sent horrible pain through his gut, Eric launched himself with all force into the woods. The dog didn't miss a beat in turning to match his direction. The chase was on.

Within seconds, Eric regretted his choice to charge headlong into a forest he knew nothing about. Riding in almost untouched forest at full speed when he barely had the skill to ride fast on pavement was insane enough. It felt downright suicidal with an apparently ravenous beast in hot pursuit.

"This is what I get for going outside," Eric managed to huff out as he pushed his untried legs harder and harder.

He kept pushing his bike as fast as his horribly out of

shape body would allow. Looking back, he saw the dog getting closer and closer. The odds of avoiding those teeth were growing more and more slim. He turned his head and eyes forward again.

"Yeaaah!" Acting on instincts he was shocked to learn he possessed, Eric lowered his head and cranked the handle bars sharply to the left and did his best to dodge a tree that seemed to leap into his path. Dust and sticks flew in the air behind him as he barely maintained control of his bike. He heard the dog growl, clearly caught up in the debris that his lucky dodge managed to toss behind him. Maybe that was the trick. Make so much of a mess that the dog wouldn't be able to keep a bead on Eric. He smiled. "Sure, and if I could actually do more than hang on for dear life, I might give that tactic a shot."

Eric leaned forward and did his best to put on the speed. He didn't even know how far into the woods this horrible chase had taken him, although he knew beyond a doubt that he was well beyond range of his mom's voice. Which was bad, and not because that meant he wouldn't hear her when it was time to come home. Oh, no. It was bad because that meant there was no way she, or anyone, would hear his likely screams of agony when the dog finally overtook him and locked that jaw firmly on the squishier bits of his body. So why he was laughing, Eric would never fully understand. Although that was his way when he was utterly and perfectly frightened. And in this case, he was just a few seconds away from breaking out into hysterics. Or, at least he would have been were he better focused on the ground farther ahead and not immediately in front. Eric never saw the raised bit of dirt that wore over a tree long ago felled by the weather. Indeed, he only had the time to let out a rare curse word that would have earned him a dinner-free night in his room before he and his prized vehicle of canine escape took to the skies. A boy and his bike were soon parted.

The world slowed down as Eric flew through the sky. It was kind of beautiful in a horrible way. He knew from all his reading that the human mind had a way of slowing down time, or, at least the perception of time. Eric had always wanted to experience that feeling; he was just profoundly upset that it was this very event that gave him his first glimpse into the world of temporal distortion. If he somehow survived this event he was going write the coolest game of all time. As the trees spun around his head, he severely doubted this would have a happy ending. In between the trees he caught glimpses of the dog. It had come to some form of halt, as if it knew nature was going to do the heavy lifting of felling its prey. The dog only needed to walk up and enjoy the fruits of Eric's poorly trained bike skills. The sky somehow grew larger as Eric began his quick descent to the hard forest floor; somewhere he heard steel and aluminum crashing into a thick bush. "Oh sure," he thought, "the thing made out of metal gets the padded landing. Me? I get rocks and teeth." And with that, his back and butt landed with such force he was certain what was left of his insides would come bursting from his mouth. Instead, only a scream that nearby neighbors would just assume was some animal getting caught in the jaws of some other predator.

"Yeaaaaaahhhhhhhh!"

He could barely move, but the pain let him know that, for now, he was alive. The dog took the scream as his cue. Tail straight and muzzle forward, the massive animal burst into action.

There was little Eric could do but put his scratched beyond belief arms in front of his face and wait for the inevitable. Eyes firmly locked shut, the sharp pain he was expecting never came. Instead the dog let out a massive yelp just as Eric felt its hot breath on his arms. Then, from out of nowhere, a voice cried out.

"Raw! Raw! RAAAAAW!!! Yeah, you better run. More of that for you. Runnnnnnnn!"

Eric didn't open his eyes. Didn't even move his arms. Strangely, the only thing he did do was wonder to himself "Who actually says 'raw-raw' these days?" As if in answer to his internal thoughts, the voice spoke to him, or at least to the heap of terror on the ground that passed for Eric .

"You okay? That was a really nasty crash."

No longer masked by auditory bravado, Eric could tell the voice belonged to a girl. An older one, but a girl no less.

"Hey, can you move? Talk?" The voice paused, clearly waiting to see if Eric would reply, and when he didn't, adding, "Um, maybe put your arms down because this is getting weird."

Eric opened his eyes and let his arms fall to his side. There, standing just a few feet away was the very same freckled girl that saw him take a massive fist to his gut no less than twenty-four hours ago. Seeing how she was dressed, he could tell why most of her face was covered in freckles. In this blinding and increasingly warm summer sun, this rather tall girl wore an outfit that looked more at home on a soccer field than a forest. Her shorts were clearly meant for someone larger, held up with a belt he could tell had a few extra holes punched in it so she could cinch it even tighter. A tank top that she didn't really wear so much as it just hung off her rather wide shoulders. Her spiky blond hair stood straight up, but not because she styled it that way, but just because that's what it wanted to do. In her right hand, she held a rock that was still in a slightly cocked position. A position that suggested at any moment she could unleash a throw that would take your head off. And considering the ravenous dog was nowhere to be seen, she was a very good aim. Eric moved his eyes to meet hers.

"Yeah, I can talk."

She smiled. "What about move?"

Eric started to shift on the dirt to stand. A stabbing pain shot up his leg and smack dab into the middle of his stomach. It was a good thing Eric still hadn't reached the age where letting out a shriek in front of a girl would give him cause to be embarrassed, because there was no stifling the yell as he fell back to the ground. The tall girl smiled again, but with more sympathy than humor.

"I guess that's my answer. Don't move, let me help you up."

Eric felt a slight twinge of pride swell up. "No. I can. I mean... I can."

She sighed to herself and starting walking toward him.

"Don't even try it. I get enough of that from the other guys. You're new, and both times I've looked at you, you've been knocked on your butt. So stop trying to impress me." Eric did as he was told and took her arm as she extended it. Although truth be told, he had no idea why she thought he wanted to impress her. Instead, he gave her a genuine smile and thanked her as she hefted him up.

"Whew, you're really strong."

She tilted her head. "Thanks. I guess." They both stood there in an awkward silence in the middle of the woods in Ashen Forest Estates.

"This is the first time I've actually seen you on your feet... You're short."

Eric let out a sigh. "My whole family's short. I'm Eric. Eric Del Bosque."

She smiled. "Welcome to Ashen Forest, Eric. I'm Heather, Heather Fos—"

Eric again fell back on his habit of speaking before thinking.

"Oh, Heather Foster. You live in the house with all the junk cars and funny mom." Heather shot him a nasty look that made him wish that dog had done him in. "You can punch me if you want."

Heather Foster just chuckled, "I should, but you aren't wrong. Yeah, Heather Foster. My mom is why I'm out here right now."

"What?"

She continued on. "Yeah, my mom said she met you yesterday. Said you were nice and caught my dog. He got out again. Anyway, when she described you I felt bad for laughing at you yesterday. Came over to apologize. I saw you ride down the street. Then, heard I old man Conner's pet Balrog take off after you."

Eric's eyes shot wide open.

"Did you just say 'Balrog?'"

Heather nodded in mock annoyance. Whatever she said

next was lost as Eric realized he might actually make a friend in this strange new place. She knew what a Balrog was. This was quickly becoming the best day ever.

"Hey, Eric! You still there"? He snapped back to attention as she poised her body as if asking him a question. Which he would soon learn, she was.

"I said, can you ride back?"

Eric stretched and felt his leg. "I think maybe I should walk it home."

"Okay, well, I'll walk back with you. If that's okay with you?"

Eric braced himself as bent over to pick up his bike. "That would be nice. Thanks."

His bike wasn't in half as bad as shape as he was. In fact, with just a little twist of the grips, you wouldn't even think the bike took as hard a fall as it had. Heather seemed to recognize this fact as she walked alongside Eric.

"That's not a bad bike. Nothing too fancy, but that also means not a lot of parts to break. Which is helpful." She poked at Eric on his left shoulder, one of the few spots on his body that amazingly didn't hurt. Well, not until that moment. This Heather girl really was stronger than she looked. Without missing a beat, she continued. "You know, for the next time you decided to send it flying into the woods." Eric just looked at the ground as the two of them slowly made their way through the woods and back toward the street. While he was never someone that felt a need to impress others, it still stung a bit to be reminded of just how horrible he was at your average kid stuff.

Possibly sensing Eric's discomfort, Heather tried to ease

his wounded ego. "Relax, everyone takes a nasty spill in these woods. It's like a right of passage. Although most of us aren't pedaling for dear life at the same time. All in all, that was some impressive riding you pulled off."

Without thinking, Eric smiled, Heather's attempt at empathy was working pretty well.

"Thanks. Also, thanks for saving my butt back there."

Heather shrugged and tossed the rock she was still holding behind them, into the trees.

"Don't mention it. Honestly, I've never seen Conner's dog act that way. I mean, Bubba isn't the nicest of animals that walks on four legs. But I've never seem him take to a person like that. He's very much a bark at the top of his lungs from the fence kind of dog. You know, all bark and all that."

Eric finally turned his attention a bit toward Heather. "Wait, the dog is really named Bubba?"

Heather chuckled. "Can you believe it? I mean, who still names their dog Bubba?"

Eric couldn't help himself. Even in his state of major pain and minor embarrassment, he let his sentence slip out. "Probably the same kind of person that yells 'raw-raw' when they're trying to scare Bubba away."

Heather wasn't going to let the joke slide. "You know, I can always go find the dog and just hold you down while he chomps on your spindly little legs."

Eric couldn't tell if she was honestly angry at him or not. And so he fell back on his other nasty habit of utter submission. Turning his head away yet again and in the lowest of voices possible, he verbally threw himself at Heather's mercy.

She laughed louder than when she saw him burst from the

barn, chased by his phantom monsters.

"Wow, Eric, you really need to lighten up! Sheesh. You're not going to last the summer if you can't take a shot now and then." He looked back up at her. "Trust me. As local kids go, I'm probably the easiest one to get along with. If you can't take a joke from me, well, it's going to be a rough few years for you." With that she pulled him in close. Awkwardly close. Holding Eric still, she started to move her hand up and down, from the top of his head to the top of hers. It wasn't the biggest gap in the world, but enough to prove her point. "Hm, that's about four inches." Eric raised his left eyebrow; even though he knew he wasn't going to be the tallest person around, it was more than a little weird to be so blatantly reminded of that fact. Heather continued. "Something tells me this little divide is always going to be here, so you need to lighten up. Take a joke. Because even though you and me are gonna be friends, I have no intention of spending my summer pulling you up from the ground. Be it from a nasty bike crash or Rusty, the neighborhood slime."

"The red head's name is Rusty"? Eric replied, really hoping she would let him go. As she finally did so, she nodded.

"Well, that's the name we hear when his dad belts it out for the whole dang forest to hear. So, sure."

They finally made it to the paved road and started the surprisingly short trip back to his house. It's amazing how much longer a trip can feel when you're pedaling for dear life. Eric needed to know more if he was going to spend so much time around all these new faces.

"So, apart from me ramming into him, why does this Rusty hate me so much?"

Heather paused a moment before she answered him.

"For starters, he doesn't really like anyone. Most of us only hang around him when we all go out for a ride. He's got his buddies, toadies really, and I've got mine." Eric nodded. Pack mentality was well known to him. Didn't matter the location; it was always the same. Heather continued.

"And you guys moving into that empty plot of land covering some of the best bike trails in the boring community of Ashen Forest Estates didn't help. I hate to say it Eric, but you broke a major rule before you ever even took one step outside."

Eric let out a whistle. "Oh, man. I didn't pick to live up here!"

Heather shrugged. "Hey, I get it. Them's the breaks. I don't hate you for it. But I'm afraid Rusty and his buddies are going to be giving you the stink eye for a good long while still. So, do your best to stay clear of them." They walked a few more paces before Heather shifted the subject.

"So, just what the heck were you doing in McCloud barn, anyway? You got a death wish or something?"

Eric paused. "I don't understand."

Heather shook her head, "I've lived here so long, I keep forgetting what's it's like to actually be the new person." Although they had made it to Eric's driveway, Heather waved him to follow her around his house and toward the barn. He followed. Something that could phase this girl was something he just had to learn more about. "Look at the barn. Notice anything strange about it?"

Eric stared hard at the barn, then back to Heather, and then the barn again. "Um, not really. No."

Heather let out a sigh. "You really never have spent time

outside, have you"?

Eric did his best to retort. "No. I mean. No. Yes. Yes, I have. Look, I had a yard when I lived in town and I even went outside during recess. I know that sounds shocking to you, but it's true."

Heather could tell she pushed him a little too hard with that one.

"Look, I didn't mean it that way. What I meant was, you've never really wandered out in nature. And I don't mean parks, playgrounds, and nice yards. I mean actual nature. With bugs and animals, great and small."

Eric had to agree, she had him with that one.

"No, not really."

Heather continued her lesson. "Okay. So, what I mean is what isn't around the barn. Granted, it's hard to see from this far away, but truth be told this is about as close as I like to get. But, if you look closely, you'll notice nothing lives in or around that barn."

Eric leaned in, as if the extra few inches would improve his view. Somehow, it did.

"Whoa. You're right. There. There isn't anything around it."

Heather nodded and continued.

"Yup, not even weeds grow around that place. Now, you ask our parents why the barn looks the way it does and they'll tell you it's because the realtors keep the place clean, so it will sell quicker. But you know what?" Eric shook his head. "It has always been that way."

Eric looked back at Heather, his face aglow with questions.

"You think it's something else?"

Heather nodded.

"I know it's something else. As does every kid that's ever lived in Ashen Forest Estates. Shoot, even before there was an Ashen Forest."

Eric looked back at the barn. With each word Heather spoke, he felt an air of eeriness overtake him.

"It's not the barn that scares everyone. It's whatever the barn is built over that keeps everyone away."

Eric stood motionless, but his mind raced with questions.

"So that barn hasn't always been there?"

Heather shrugged again, not that Eric was paying that much attention.

"It's been here for as long as I've been alive. And, it's been there since the McClouds' kids went off to college, and stayed once the McClouds themselves moved away. But Mr. Conner once told my mom that when he was a kid, way before the McClouds ever moved to Ashen Forest, that is a stone building. A stone building made from lava rocks tossed into the air from the last time Grizzly Mountain erupted."

Eric had done a bit of research before he moved up here and knew that it had been well over a century since the volcano erupted. His eyes widened and let slip out a word that would have earned him a quick slap on the wrist and no dinner. Heather didn't flinch; she simply agreed.

"You said it. new kid."

Eric turned back to Heather. "Wait, does that mean people have lived up here for over a hundred years?"

Heather shook her head with far more certainty than he was comfortable with.

"Not people. At least not like you and I."

Eric's eyes grew wider still. "What do you mean, 'not people'?"

Heather leaned in a little close to Eric. Of all the answers she could have given him, the one that she said was by far the answer he liked the least.

"No idea."

Eric turned back to face her.

"Come on. Now I know you're just messing with me. Ha-ha, very funny. Get the new kid all worked up." Yet something on Heather's face told him that she wasn't messing with him. Something told him that for all her apparent bravado, she didn't like being this close to the barn. Or rather, she didn't like being around whatever the local kids believed was trapped inside, or under, that barn.

"The real reason nothing alive comes near that barn is because nothing can."

Eric looked confused at her statement.

"Wait a second, I went inside. I assure you, I am very much alive."

Heather didn't have a real answer, but that didn't stop her from replying.

"Beats me. Maybe you weren't there long enough. Maybe you're too big; I mean, even your small size is bigger than the average spider or mouse."

Eric still wasn't buying it.

"And I suppose that's the same reason for the cat being alive as well."

Heather shrugged again.

"Like I said, maybe you just got lucky. Lucky that he wasn't awake and hungry."

Eric had had enough.

"Okay, I give. I was lucky who wasn't hungry?"

With a flick of her leg, Heather flicked up the kickstand to her bike. She shivered a bit. "You still don't get it, do you? Since before any kid can remember, something has stood over that patch of land. The adults don't talk about it, but even they don't go near the place when the sun goes down."

Something in Heather's voice was causing Eric to worry just a little. Maybe she wasn't just messing around with the new kid like he was hoping. She continued on.

"When you guys moved up here, this area of Ashen Forests was completely free. Sure, we ran our bikes around it and played around. But, we never disturbed whatever is buried under that barn."

Eric raised his hands.

"Hey, I didn't do anything! We just moved here!"

Heather put her hand on his shoulder.

"I know. But before they dropped this house over our favorite trails, they had to dig. With big ol' tractors and backhoes. Tractors that shook the land and backhoes that might have dug a little too deep." She leaned over and pointed toward a specific place under the barn. The very same place Eric saw a sickly green glow and heard shrieks emanate in the night. "Large machinery that sent shockwaves under the, until recently, undamaged stone floor."

Eric kept moving his head between the spot and Heather. Heather and the spot.

"Oh, no."

Heather nodded.

"Oh, no is right." She stood back up and turned to ride back to her place. "Sorry buddy, but it looks like you put a crack in his cage."

Eric turned as she rode across the street.

"Whose cage?!"

She didn't even look back to answer as she rode behind her house.

"Hairy Baby."

Eric turned back to the barn.

"Wait. Hairy what?"

7
A TRIP TO TOWN

That night Eric dreamed of strange creatures that stalked his forested home. As dreams went, it wasn't wholly displeasing. His dream self was no small boy that wasted energy simply drawing breath after a long run, nor was he some muscle-bound character from a superhero comic. Instead, when Eric closed his eyes and his mind wandered into the dreamscape, in his place stood a learned hero. The proud champion that would rather talk his way out of a bind, but wasn't short on some combat skills were words not enough. Years of reading epic tales of adventure and fantasy were the fuel with which his rich mind powered these nocturnal adventures. And so, for all the strangeness and danger his real life had already faced, it was nice to close his eyes and not dream of shrieks in the night or nasty neighborhood bullies beating him to a pulp. At least that's how he remembers his dream starting.

All too soon his visions shifted. The creatures of fancy gave way to horrendous images of possession and distortion. Even

Eric himself had shifted. Gone was the strong hero that allowed him to travel his own dreams without a care. He was simply the new kid that didn't stand a chance against Rusty and his sidekick, to say nothing of whatever was now infecting his pleasant vision. The animals all began to change; twisted and horrible, they came at Eric. But none was worse than the massive beast that slowly formed before him. Its teeth jutted from its mouth at unnatural angles as green ichor dripped from its maw. Eric couldn't tell, but part of him swore that he heard the beast say something to him. Even though he knew this wasn't real, that it was just a dream, Eric felt a fear run through his core like he'd never experienced. A fear he didn't think was possible. Again the beast started to speak. He didn't understand a word the beast said, but the intent was clear. He meant to take them all. Beneath his feet, Eric found the ground begin to shake. Cracks broke in the ground as green light burst from below. The beast howled as the ground shook more and more violently. Eric let out a cry. The horrible vision left his mind as his eyes burst open. Still he cried out as the ground just kept shaking.

What few things he'd set out in his room vibrated and fell to the floor.

"Mom! MOM!" was all Eric could cry as he sat up in bed. Just as his mother threw his bedroom door open, the shaking stopped.

"Mijo! Shhhh. It's okay. It's okay. We just had a small rumble. Are you alright? Didn't anything hit you?"

Eric was still visibly shaken as his mom sat next to him and held his shoulders. Slowly, he started to collect himself.

"I'm. I'm okay. I just never felt that before. Sorry."

A TRIP TO TOWN

Earlina held her son a little longer, feeling his breathing slow to a safe pace.

"It's okay. I grew up with them, and even I never got used to them. I don't think you're supposed to."

Eric looked back at his mom.

"I didn't think they happened here."

Earlina looked back at her son.

"I didn't think so either, but I guess that volcano isn't as dormant as everyone says." She looked at his room, most of it still unpacked. "Not that it seems to affect this place. Come on, Eric, you need to unpack, or a small earthquake will be the least of your concerns."

Eric smiled; although it was an admonishment, it was also his mom's playful way of letting him know that everything was going to be okay. He leaned back against his headboard and cringed, unable to hide his pain.

"Now what?" asked his mom. Eric knew there was no reason in hiding anything; she would find out. Better to get it over with now. With that, Eric rambled on about his first bike adventure through the neighborhood, and all that it entailed. To her credit, Earlina kept rather calm.

Eric spent the bulk of Sunday in his house. The standard rule in regards to unlocking the treasure chest allowed for such days of rest. And even if he was in the mood to explore his new neighborhood some more, his mom would have none of it. There was simply no hiding the various bumps, bruises, and cuts that covered every part of his body that hadn't been protected the day before. And really, had he allowed his mom to pry even further, she would have found more. Also the fact that his mom had seen his new friend, the tall and rather outspoken Heather Foster, help him back to his yard the day prior, didn't help matters.

"Eric, I'm really glad you're making friends, but could you maybe not attach various injuries to each new acquaintance? At this rate you'll be in a body cast by the fourth of July." Still, there was no hiding the happiness in her voice. Sure, he was a bit worse for wear, but he was getting out there. Eric was indeed experiencing life, complete with all its dangers. What his mom couldn't possibly foresee were the events of this day that would set into motion a situation would almost cost Eric, his new friend, and everyone in Ashen Forest Estates their lives.

Just as his mom had promised the Friday before, they packed up the busted but wholly reliable family car for a trip into town. Not that this time of year required any kind of special packing, but his mom had spent enough time on the side of the road due to all manner of events this region of the state could throw at you that she was never unprepared. From an outsider's perspective it was a little strange. But this was Grizzlydale; it was a town of strange. You stood out if you didn't treat even the simplest of outings like an explorer facing a new land.

With the car packed and prepared, Earlina popped back in the house and asked Eric if he was ready.

"Eric, I wrote down the two places in town that teach karate. Pick which one sounds the best and we'll stop by before we hit the grocery store."

Eric shouted something from his bathroom that was, even with the best of parental hearing, unintelligible. His mom was not amused. "At least spit before you try and shout from back there, jeez! Or, maybe trying finishing and then come out and speak to your mother like a real human being."

To that, Eric did indeed step out into the hall, minty fresh toothpaste still dripping from his jaw and likely staining his freshly cleaned shirt. At least this one would match the others.

"But if I waited to reply, you'd be annoyed that I didn't answer you right away."

His mom still had her back to him.

"You're right, so as soon as you realize you can't win, you will have a better..." His mom turned to face him, keys in her hand. "Dang it, boy! I just washed those. Great, well, at least this one will match the others."

Eric's eyes widened. This was the second adult in about a week that clearly had insight into his inner thoughts. He stood there, pondering if this was a gift he would one day grow into. Or, was it something only girls possessed? He'd have to ask Heather, assuming she was old enough to develop such powers. With frightening clarity, his mom continued. "Yes, I can tell what you're thinking. And no, I can't read minds. You're just a slob like your dad, so I have experience. Now, rinse up and come outside. We need to get a move on."

Eric nodded. He was still going to ask Heather.

"Hey, mom." Eric wiped the last of the toothpaste from his mouth and walked out to meet his mother. "Mom, um. Can we stop by the library when we're in town?"

His mom had her hand on the car door handle, her body slumped just a little as she knew this was the beginning of his attempt to get out of karate classes. Classes he himself requested not three days before.

"I thought you wanted to take karate?"

Eric shuffled his way to the car. "Well... Not really. I mean. I wanted to read some things. And, well, you said I wanted to."

"And you don't?"

Eric lowered his head. It was time to let this one out. "I just didn't want to argue. It was easier to let you think that."

His mom flung open the car door and jumped in with a phrase that he didn't fully understand, but knew it was up there with things adults said that even older kids didn't say around their parents. It was the worst possible mix of annoyance with a side of disappointment. Eric was going to have to think and talk fast if he wanted out of this one.

"I mean. I like the idea of karate, I just, um."

His mom cut him off.

"Forget it. First, yes, we can stop by the library." The annoyance slowly slipped and gave way to a general malaise that he only heard from his mom when she was talking about various family members that caused more headache than happiness. Which was the kind of person he never wanted to be. It was really amazing how quickly the shift in emotions could affect him and his mom.

"Eric, I need you to stop lying."

Eric tried to respond that it wasn't a lie, that he just let her hear what she wanted to hear. His mom wasn't going to let this one go.

"It's the same thing, letting someone believe what isn't true. You need to learn that or what few friends you are making won't stick around." Eric hopped in the car. This was going to be a serious ride into town. "You're a smart kid. So

A TRIP TO TOWN

smart that sometimes I worry you think you can talk your way out of or through anything." She started up the car. "One day it's not going to work. And when that day comes, you aren't going have time to ask why or explain your way around it. It will just hit you upside the head and there will be no going back. Do you understand me?"

Eric nodded. Quite sincerely, he said, "I think so. I just. I didn't want to hurt your feelings."

She noted the sincerity. "I know, mijo. I know. But I'd rather you just be honest from the beginning. I might get angry, but I'll get over it and we can move on. But the lying, by words or inaction, that's not so easy."

Eric sat quietly as they drove down the mountain. It was a pretty drive. Looking deep into the woods, Eric could imagine himself getting lost in the great pines that had risen from the ground over the centuries, or the boulders shot out in mere moments from the various volcanic blasts of the past. He wondered what it was like, to see the massive rocks come crashing from the sky for the first time. They rounded the corner and officially left the area known as Ashen Forest Estates and continued down the poorly maintained highway. Grizzlydale was only ten miles away, not that long of a drive when it came to a land where traveling was measured by hours, not miles. The car moved along. Signs pointed out various areas that Eric hoped to visit before the summer was out: Devil's Ranch, Humbug River, Green Rift Ravine. Places with names that conjured all manner of adventure and excitement. Looking back toward his mom, he cleared his throat. Now was as good as time as ever to go back to the very topic which opened this rather emotional can of worms.

"So, about the library."

His mom sighed.

"Yes, we can stop there. But don't think you've found a way around our little going outside for books challenge."

Eric shook his head. "Nope. Not at all. Honest. I just want to look a few things up about our neighborhood. Heather told me about some weird stuff and I want to see if the papers or books about the town ever mention it."

His mom smiled. If getting her son to imagine his neighborhood was once a hotbed of mystery got him outside more with his new friend, she wasn't going to fight it.

"Okay, that we can do. I might even let you check out a book on the area if they have one."

Eric smiled. Maybe this summer wasn't going to be so bad after all.

8
THE KEEPER OF THE BOOKS

To an outsider passing through, Grizzlydale was just another sleepy small town in rural America. And make no mistake, the town was indeed just that. However, the town had more than its share of secrets, more than you'd expect for a town that had managed to keep its population around five thousand for the better share of six decades. Family names went back far in the town, so far you'd be right in wondering how the population didn't rise or fall. The Del Bosques were an anomaly in the town of Grizzlydale. Although they'd been in the town for as long as Eric could remember, the bulk of the locals still considered them newcomers, or "flatlanders" as the saying went. And it didn't really matter how many times Eric's parents reminded the locals that they were actually from a mountain city; they were from a city, and city folks were flatlanders. Period, end of story. It was something Eric took with a grain of salt. In the grand scheme of names he'd been called in his short existence on this planet, "flatlander" was one of the better and less inflammatory ones.

Still, it was nice to go somewhere where Eric didn't feel the judgmental eyes of locals. One of those rare havens within Grizzlydale was the library, the Municipal Public Library to be specific. For as long as anyone could remember, the library occupied the building that at one time had been the frontier jail. As libraries went, this hall of knowledge was rather imposing. Standing in one of the older areas of the town, the library was flanked on all sides by examples of Grizzlydale's colorful past. Its closest neighbor was the now defunct County Courthouse. Long ago having moved to a larger location within the state, the massive building had a design that Eric had seen in many of his Greek mythology books. Massive pillars surrounded the building, made of light brown stone carved from the very foundation of the town upon which it would dispense justice. Now the Courthouse was but an empty husk, a place for kids to dare each other to spend the night, surrounded by every urban legend known to youths of all ages: Satanic cults, escaped mental patients, even a portal to haunted dimensions. They all laid claim to that large stone building. Although Eric found all of these legends to be exciting, especially the one about the Courthouse containing a portal, he mainly felt sadness when he looked at it, as if the building was a once-great hero that no one cared about anymore. Still standing proud, she was ready to serve again if anyone would just give her the chance.

Across the street from the library was the one location that did stick out. In an area of town dedicated to the past, this house almost demanded attention with its modern look and design. He heard his mom talk about what a shame it was that the new owner tore down the old building. She always mumbled the same thing whenever they stopped by: "They didn't need to burn it." Each time Eric asked her what she meant by that and each time she replied with the same answer. "What? Oh, nothing, Eric. I forgot what I was talking about." This time was no different. Eric made a mental note. One day he would ask the question before she made the comment. For now, he was content to let the question bounce around in his head. Personally, he thought the new house looked rather interesting. It had wires all over and looked more at place in his sci-fi comics than a sleepy rural town.

Behind the library was the first cemetery, the First Tyr Memorial Gardens. Even at his young age he thought this was an incredibly fancy name for a place to bury your dead. Not that such places couldn't have grand names, but it seemed like a name better reserved for national monuments, or other areas of great importance. Here? On the outer edge of what was once old Grizzlydale? Well, it was just weird. However, there was no denying that it was one of the more beautiful locations in the town. Even though his parents thought it was morbid and perhaps borderline disturbing to hear their child talk about graves, Eric would often tell them how he'd like to be buried in First Tyr Memorial Gardens. "Not that I am in any hurry or anything. But the place is just so pretty." His mom would shake her head and remind him that it was bad luck to talk of death in such a flippant manner. Eric never quite understood that. He never felt like he was celebrating the loss of life or loved ones. He just saw a place that people took time and care into cultivating and making beautiful. Okay, maybe it was a little creepy, but that didn't stop it from being a nice place to walk past on the way into the library.

Everyone did, with the parking lot being placed between the cemetery and library.

The library itself was no less interesting than its neighbors. Although the building no longer contained the absolute worst the town had to offer, each wall still had its original bars securely set into stone. Unlike most modern buildings, or even older ones after restoration, the library had but two entrances. The first was the grand steps flanked by two massive oak trees that led up into the main hall, If the stories were true, those oak trees did more than simply add a bit of nature to the surroundings. With each tree revealing unnaturally bent limbs, the stories of both trees being the sites of the town's hangings for decades seemed all too plausible. As he and his mom approached the library, she could see Eric's mind racing as he looked at the massive oaks that cast a foreboding shadow over all who approached the building.

"I know what you're thinking, and for the last time, they did not hang hundreds of people at these trees."

Eric still wasn't buying it.

"Then why won't anything grow at the base of the trees, mom? You know there are some legends that say a dead man's soul can kill life around it."

Earlina was not amused. "First off, I really don't like it when you talk that way. Second, there is no such legend; you made it up. And third, you've met the groundskeeper. He's a little crazy about weeds. Look around. Nothing grows in front of the library."

Eric shook his head.

"Then why haven't the oaks died too?"

Earlina gave up. It was better to sometimes give in to her

son's rather active mind than to argue with it logically. "Because you're right. All the dead bodies that they just left on the ground soaked into the dirt and nothing will grow."

Eric knew she was messing with him, but that'd didn't stop him from taking a rather deep breath through his nose, sticking out his chest and proclaiming, "I knew it."

Then there was the matter of the other door, on the other side of the library. In its original capacity as the jail, the other door was merely the opening local law enforcement officers would use. And, on the rare occasion when a person wasn't leaving in a pinewood box, a way to sneak offenders into the night and towards whatever direction their fate lay. Just as Eric knew the real reason no plants grew under the massive oaks, so too did he understand the other door's true purpose. If the stories were true, and Eric had no reason to believe they weren't, the second entrance into the Grizzlydale Public Library was more than just an employee entrance. This was the door that led to the hidden vaults. The vaults were where the oldest of Grizzlydale residents kept their secrets, and, scarier still, where they kept the people that were too evil for even the oaks out front to deal with. As she did so many times, Earlina noticed Eric staring off into the great nothing, almost looking through the library. She knew immediately what he was thinking.

"Why must everything have some form of sinister secret attached to it? It's just the back entry to the library, just like it was the back entry to the jail when the place first opened. Just stop."

Eric turned to look at his mother, his eyes seeming to sink back into his head just a little as he tried to think of ways to convince her he knew the truth. All he could come up with was a rather pathetic, "Nuh-uh."

His mom wasn't going to feed into his imagination this time.

"It's not a portal. It's not a gateway. It's a door. Look, if you're going to live in your fantasy world this much, maybe it's not a good idea to go inside. Maybe we just get the groceries and we head home. I really don't want to be on the road if we get some kind of aftershock from this morning's rumble. Something tells me this small town isn't well equipped at dealing with a real quake."

Eric smiled the most innocuous smile he had. "Mom, I'm just messing with you. I know it's not real, but it's fun to pretend. Didn't you ever pretend when you were a kid?"

His mom didn't hesitate in telling him that of course she did.

"But I also didn't let myself get so lost that my parents wondered if I was ever going to come back. Mijo, sometimes you just need to be okay with life being a little boring. Not always, but sometimes."

Eric knew his mom meant well, and, if he was being honest with himself, he really didn't believe half the stuff he heard from other kids, or what he thought of in his own mind. Even if he did think the town would be far more interesting if they were. "Now, hurry, I want to get home in time to have something beyond a pot of noodles or frozen pizza for dinner."

Eric nodded, and together they opened the barred door and entered the library.

Even by Eric's standards, the library was a strange place.

His mother clearly thought the same thing as he, but for different reasons voiced her own concern. "I still can't get used to this place. I mean, using the old jail is one thing, but you'd think they would take out the cells and just make it one large room. You know?"

Eric was only half paying attention. Just because he found something strange didn't mean he wasn't absolutely in love with it. Smiling, he looked back at his mom.

"I was just wondering why more places didn't look like this. This place is so cool!"

His mom merely shook her head.

"I really don't know where you get it from. Sure as heck not me or your father."

Eric made a face of mock disapproval.

"Your father or I, mom; father or I."

His mom gave him a loving whop upon the back of his head, "Now that, you get from me," she continued smiling at her son.. "Now hurry. We really need to get to the store".

Eric made his way to the card catalog and smiled. His school had long ago done away with this analog form of looking up books. Everything was computer based. Just like looking for articles on the Internet, if you wanted a certain book from the school library, you typed it in and this funny little cartoon character popped up and told you where to find it. They even had this animated map that showed you where to walk. For better or worse the town budget wasn't as kind to the local library as it was to his school. They had a few computers, but those were only for checking books in and out. If they were attached to any form of communication cables, it was so they could print out forms on paper that still required you to tear it carefully at the perforation points. Eric didn't mind, though. He liked going through the catalog system. It gave his task a sense of quest, like he was digging through layers of history. Even at his young age, he wondered just how many other people had stood at that very spot, how many fingers gently danced over the thick pulped paper, looking for just the right title, a stumpy pencil firmly locked between their teeth because they needed both hands to hold their place in the catalog and shift around. So lost in thought as he delved through the catalog, Eric didn't even realize that even in this silent building, he was again speaking to himself.

"I wonder if only really old people truly understand the beauty of this library?" From behind him, Eric heard a reply that caused him to jump, just a little.

"No. You don't. Although seeing me is not going to change your mind."

Eric slipped the tiny #2 pencil into his last spot so he wouldn't lose his place and turned to see whom he'd likely just annoyed by accidentally calling them old.

Behind him stood Mr. Gregory, the head librarian and to Eric's knowledge, the keeper of the best head of "mad scientist" hair he had ever seen. Even his mom joked once that Mr. Gregory must stick his hand in an electrical socket every morning to get his hair to do that. Eric knew enough about family lines to understand that while he was probably never going to bald, nor would he ever be blessed with such an awesome head of hair. Without knowing, Eric had a massive grin that Mr. Gregory was not going to let go without a comment. "You'd think by now people would stop finding it funny." He patted his, for lack of a better term, bouncy white hair. "Then again."

Eric let his smile drop a bit.

"I hope I wasn't being too loud."

Mr. Gregory leaned over Eric to see what he was looking at.

"No. In fact, I tend to think most people over react to the whole 'keep it down' rule the first librarian established ages past." Eric nodded a bit. "I was just passing by and wanted to see if you needed any help. But, from what I can see, you're pretty good at this thing."

Eric beamed with pride. He was indeed pretty good. Without even hesitating, he added, "Yeah, Dewey or Library of Congress. I can read both."

Mr. Gregory raised an equally bushy eyebrow. "Can you, now? Consider me impressed. Well, then, I won't bother you anymore, but please feel free to ask if you have any questions."

Eric's mom, looking at her phone and seeing the time, popped over and asked the wild-haired librarian if he could help her son out. She had a schedule to keep and no matter how happy she was to see her son come into his element among all the books, she had things to do.

"Actually, Mr. Gregory, my son is looking for books on the history of the town. Specifically, he wants to know more about the area that is now Ashen Forest Estates."

The librarian nodded, while Eric merely looked annoyed that his mom decided to step in and take over. He would have found the book on his own, but he guessed her schedule meant more than his desire to do it himself. Mr. Gregory looked down at Eric and saw the annoyance on his face. Thankfully, his comically crazy hair blocked Earlina's view of her own son, wearing a look she would not have taken too kindly to. Mr. Gregory said, "Well, there are certainly all manner of books and articles on the location. Are you looking for historical accounts? Or maybe some personal journals; we've managed to acquire a few from that period. Reproductions of course; the originals are locked away. To keep them safe, you understand."

Earlina shifted a bit so she could get a good look at her son.

"Well, what would you like?"

Eric was in no hurry to get back into the car and go grocery shopping just yet, so he did what all kids did best. He stalled.

"Um... Maybe. I don't know. I guess journals. But no one lived there when they made journals."

His mom rolled her eyes.

"Really, Eric? Come on, just let Mr. Gregory find you a book and let's go."

Mr. Gregory stood up and smiled at Eric's mom. "Tell you what, Mrs. Del Bosque, leave Eric here while you go run your errands. He and I can dig through all these books and see if we can find something interesting."

His mom hesitated for a moment. It was well known that Mr. Gregory was a respected and trusted member of the town. She smiled.

"Why do I feel like I am being played by a couple of bookworms that just want to get a troublesome mother out of the picture?" Mr. Gregory and Eric looked at each other and mockingly shrugged their shoulders. She continued, "I have no ally in this, do I?"

Mr. Gregory and Eric smiled at her. She shook her head, but smiled at her son. "If he's gets to be a pain, please call me."

Mr. Gregory laughed just loud enough to attract the attention of an elderly lady reading her magazine; he covered his mouth. "It's no trouble. I only wish there were more kids like your son. It will be my pleasure."

Eric smiled at his mom. "Thanks."

His mom mumbled "Sure, sure," under her breath and then quite sternly told her son that she would be back in two hours and he better be waiting for her outside. She didn't even want to get out of the car to get him. Eric smiled again and made a promise that he truly intended to keep. With that, his mom shook Mr. Gregory's hand and went to run her errands.

Mr. Gregory and Eric watched her drive away. With Earlina completely out of sight, Mr. Gregory turned to face Eric.

"Now then, what are we really trying to learn about"?

Eric smiled back at the librarian. "Actually, exactly what my mom said I was looking for." Eric turned backed to the card catalog, his finger still holding a place. "I really do want to know more about the town. Well, at least my area of it."

Mr. Gregory looked a little bothered by the rather mundane truth, but simply shrugged his shoulders and looked at the section Eric was saving.

"So, local history. Well, like I said, you're in the right spot. Are you looking for natural history or town history."

Eric wasn't entirely sure of the answer to that. Part of him wanted to yell out that he wanted to know about all the strange myths and legends he'd always heard about Grizzlydale. But specifically, he wanted to know about this "Hairy Baby" monster Heather told him was trapped in a stone slab in the all too perfect barn that was only thirty feet from his bedroom window. Eric paused, wondering if there was any way he could bring up such a concept without sounding like a complete freak. He really didn't want to become the very person his mom was so desperately trying to get him not to be—the town crazy. Eric tightened his face in mock concentration, scratched his head in an attempt to lure the correct phrase out from his brain and said the very first thing that came to him.

"Town history, I guess."

Almost immediately a voice in his head scolded him for not just spitting out what he really wanted to know. But, the die had been cast and the search was on. Besides, it wasn't like he could just go back to digging on his own. And with Mr. Gregory helping him, he could find the basic stuff quickly, giving him all the more time to look for the weird stuff.

Mr. Gregory nodded. "That's easy enough." Taking a note of the numbers on the cards, Mr. Gregory wrote them down on a slip of scrap paper and told Eric to follow him. He did so without question, all but entranced by the way the librarian's hair seemed to bounce with life of its own with each step. Eric found himself stifling a chuckle as he imagined the librarian twisting miniature springs into his hair each morning, guaranteeing optimal boing with every step he took. If Mr. Gregory sensed the extra attention he was receiving from his young customer, he wasn't going to show it. Turning the corner and down to the 900s, or cellblock G for those that were old enough to remember, Mr. Gregory found some of the books Eric would want for his research.

"Here you go. This pretty much covers everything about this town from the very first settlers to just before World War II. We'll have to go a section over if you want something later." Eric took the books in his hands and stared at them a little too long before thanking the man. Mr. Gregory noticed the odd delay.

"Are you sure this is what you're looking for, son?" Eric again snapped out of his slight daze and looked at the librarian.

"Oh, um. Yes. Thank you. Um, this is what I wanted. Sure." There was a slight pause as Mr. Gregory looked at him. Eric knew he felt there was something else going on. However, unlike most adults Eric knew, Mr. Gregory was going to take him at his word. At least for now. "Okay, then. Well, it's going to be a bit before your mom comes back. Feel free to take these to any of the desks and start poring over them. Leave the ones you don't need on the desk and we'll check out the ones you do. Sound good?"

Eric smiled. "Sounds good."

Mr. Gregory started to walk back to the main counter, seeing another patron needing his services. Only taking a few steps, Eric asked one more question.

"Actually, is there anything going back older? Anything about the people that lived here before the settlers?"

Mr. Gregory turned and smiled. "Same section, but a few shelves down." Eric nodded, this time with genuine thanks. It still wasn't everything he wanted. But it was a good place to start. With that, Eric found a few more books on the earliest people of the area and found himself a nice quiet place to read.

Time passed at an almost magic pace for Eric as he pored over the various books on the desk. Looking up from the pages, he realized what felt like minutes had nearly been an hour. He rubbed his eyes and looked around the library. No changes. Everything was where he'd seen it when he and his mom first stepped inside. Looking back at his books, he realized with frustration that he was no closer to the answer he sought than before. "Come on, there has to be an answer somewhere. I mean, who keeps up a legend of a monster for all this time and never once thinks to write it in a darn history book?" A gentle shush from a cell block over let Eric know that perhaps his frustrations were becoming a bit too public. Closing the text on "County Land Purchases, 1858—1925" he removed his glasses and gave his eyes a solid rubbing. Taking a page from almost every movie montage he ever saw, Eric stepped away from the desk and stretched his arms and legs as he paced about.

"It's the first week of my summer vacation and here I am hanging out in a library, checking to see if there is some special book titled 'Hey Eric, the Monsters are Here.' Wow, that sounds pathetic, even by my lowered standards." He stopped pacing and stood behind the chair that he just spent the better part of an hour sitting upon. "Maybe Heather was just cracked in the head. I mean, maybe she does believe there is some nasty creature locked away next to my room. Doesn't mean she isn't playing a joke on me." Something in that final statement gave Eric pause. He leaned on the back of the chair and stared intently at the books before him. He murmured to himself, "Cracked."

Sitting back down with far more intent and purpose that needed, Eric gathered all the books in a nice, neat pile. With a bit too much fervor, he started flipping through each and every book.

"Dates. Dates. Let's see. Yup, this one starts at 1858. So does this one. Okay, let's keep looking. Whoa. Okay." Eric turned to the book on the original Native American population. "There it is, right there. The volcano. Everything about the native people of the region stopped the year before the eruption; all the books on the settlers start the year after." Eric's mind raced at what that could mean. While he knew life was by no means perfect in old Grizzlydale, he also knew it wasn't horrible. In fact, to hear old timers talk, the pioneer people from the East and the native tribes got along fairly well. There is no history, biased or otherwise, that listed any real confrontation. It was one of the few places in the American West that really did have enough room for everyone. "Then why they heck won't either history say what happened that year?" Lost in his discovery, Eric didn't notice Mr. Gregory had again walked up to the desk where he was reading.

"Because that's when the first Tyr opened up and Grizzlydale stopped being a normal town."

Eric froze in his seat. There was a tone to the librarian's voice that Eric wasn't comfortable with. It wasn't dangerous, but also definitely not something he'd ever heard or felt before. Slowly, Eric turned in his seat to look at Mr. Gregory.

"The first what? The first tear?" Eric sheepishly asked, trying to ignore the idea that the library was actually growing darker.

"Not tear. Tyr."

Eric's mind raced as he realized the librarian said the word as it matched the cemetery outside. Mr. Gregory closed the books on the desk and smiled. "Your mom is going to be here any second. Before you wait for her outside, why don't you tell me what you're really looking for."

Eric looked around. Mr. Gregory didn't look threatening, but there was a strange air to him. A power that both frightened and excited Eric.

"I saw a green light in the ground. Outside. Next to my room. Everyone is afraid of it."

Mr. Gregory squinted and tightened his lips.

"But not you?"

Eric shook his head.

"No. But I think I should be."

Mr. Gregory smiled, although Eric was certain it was the dimming light, he saw an eerie glow from within what was once the kind, if a tad bizarre, librarian.

"That remains to be seen, lad, but I've got a good feeling about you."

Eric was about to respond when he felt a rise in the temperature around him. With the feeling of warmth came a general illumination to the library once again. He quickly looked around the room and then back to Mr. Gregory. Although still uncomfortably close to Eric, any feeling of unease was gone. In its place was the warm smile he saw whenever he visited the Grizzlydale Public Library. Mr. Gregory smiled again.

"Sounds like your mom is here."

Eric shook his head in confusion.

"Huh?" His confusion was answered by two rapid honks of a car horn and a declaration from outside.

"Eric! Come on! I told you to be waiting outside!"

Mr. Gregory helped Eric up from the chair and walked him outside.

"My fault, Mrs. Del Bosque, your son was helping me and I lost track of time."

Eric's mom softened a bit at the news, although she was clearly in no mood to linger and chat.

"Ah, well, that's okay. Come on mijo, lets head home and unload the groceries." Eric hopped into the car. As they drove away all he could see was Mr. Gregory, smiling and waving as they disappeared down the road.

"And you didn't even check out a book. Well, I'm glad you used all that time wisely."

Eric didn't answer as they drove home.

Back up the mountain.

Back to the first Tyr, whatever that meant.

9
THE MISSING DOG

It had been a few days since Eric had had his strange encounter at the Grizzlydale Public Library. He just kept running the events over and over in his head. Nothing made any sense. In the beginning, he started to convince himself he had imagined the whole thing. There was no way the kind and informative librarian began speaking in strange tones as the very fabric of the building shifted. It had to be something else. And yet every night since their little chat, when Eric closed his eyes, he heard Mr. Gregory's voice fill his dreams.

"I have a good feeling about you."

Each time Eric woke up in a dark bedroom, convinced he wasn't alone. This night was no different as he pulled the blankets tighter over his body, bringing the edge of the blankets to just above his jaw. It was early summer in Grizzlydale and while the hottest days of the year were still a couple months away, it was by no means cold enough to warrant such a thick covering. Still, a bit of uncomfortable warmth was well worth the protection a blanket handmade by his grandma provided. It was indeed a universal fact that whatever waited for you in the dark had no powers against such totems of loving care and warmth. Eric mumbled a faint "Thanks, grandma" as he slid himself lower into his bed.

Sleep would not return to Eric that night. Instead he just laid in his bed, his senses keenly aware of any shift in sight or sound. There were more than a few moments that night when Eric swore the very walls of his room shimmered in the eerie glow provided by the moon outside. He was tempted to sneak out into the living room and watch some television to drown out his own growing fears. "Except there is no volume low enough that I won't wake up mom, and she'd just be annoyed and send me right back to my room. So forget that idea, Eric. You have to make it until sunrise." What he didn't add to his out-loud conversation was the real reason he didn't want to slip out into the living room. Doing so would require he step into the darkness, his feet sliding out from the protective barrier of his bed and onto the floor, a floor that allowed for a painfully large space between it and the bed. A space where his active mind was absolutely certain that whatever Mr. Gregory had hinted at was waiting for him to expose his ankles. And then, that would be it for Eric . Cut down by night creatures before his time. No sir, he would wait out the darkness. Even if it meant going another day with baggy eyes and dark circles around them.

That evidence of poor sleep was making it harder and harder to keep his mom at bay. Just as she was certain that any random injury could lead to debilitating disability if ignored, dark circles under one's eyes was a sure sign of rampaging allergies, so deadly they could cause one's entire body to break out in a rash and likely explode at any given moment. In a way, Eric actually hoped he wouldn't be able to hide his growing fatigue from his mom. While it meant another round of nasty Mentholatum rub on his chest, back, and neck, it also meant some allergy pills, which had a wonderful side effect of causing Eric to drift into sleep. If he could pull that off during the day, maybe all his problems would be over.

"Unless it doesn't matter if it's day or night. What if whatever Mr. Gregory hinted at can get me whenever I fall asleep?"

The thought made Eric's mind race even more and curse himself for sneaking in a viewing of that horror movie with the guy with knife fingers. It was easy to tell himself it was all fake. Until he was the kid trying not to fall asleep. His random thoughts took his mind away from the general fear that was constantly floating just under his all-too-vocal thoughts. In time he saw the gentle orange rays of the morning sun break through the dense pine forest and into his room. As always, he poked his head out a little further and took in his room. While he still hadn't made a real dent in unpacking his belongings, everything was at least where he left them the day before. With the sun fully up, he slipped from his bed and walked out to the scent of his mom's morning coffee. She still wouldn't let him drink any, convinced it would stunt his growth. Eric found that hilarious, as he was fairly certain that slice of genetic destiny was fulfilled when his rather short father married his even shorter mother. While Eric only had the scientific knowledge of a boy entering fifth grade, he was pretty sure a pair of long pants was not in his future. Still, he did enjoy the smell and it always made him smile. What was waiting for him on the kitchen table did not.

"Morning. Whew, I would ask how you slept, but those circles under your eyes tell me the whole story." Just as he thought, his mom hadn't missed a beat. Doing his best to pretend like he was fine, Eric yawned and plopped himself at the kitchen table.

"I'm fine, mom. Just had a weird dream that woke me up and I wasn't able to get back to sleep."

His mom nodded; for now, this was good and really wasn't at all untrue. "Okay, well, try and get to bed early tonight." Eric returned the nod as another yawn escaped him. Earlina stood up to pour herself another cup of coffee, as she did so, so slipped a flyer toward Eric.

"Mrs. Foster left this in our mailbox. Have you talked with Heather at all about it?" The flier showed a couple of badly taken photos of Heather's massive dog, the very same animal that looked like it was going to send Eric flying on his first day in the neighborhood. The same dog that had instead halted in its tracks by the barn that was giving Eric the willies now. The same dog that, over the past couple of weeks, Eric had grown to actually like. He was big and dumb, but it was hard to hate the wanton zeal with which the dog approached everything. That, and the nearly endless supplies of bandanas Heather dressed the poor pooch in. The flier read:

"Missing–Hoss–Last seen on River Drive in Ashen Forest Estates. Don't be scared by size. Hoss is very nice and his family misses him. Please call. Reward if found"

Eric shook his head.

"I had no idea. But that would explain why I haven't seen Heather around the past few days."

His mom sat back down.

"After breakfast, why don't you go over and see if you can help her." Although this was one of his mom's famous non-request requests, Eric was all-too-willing to help. He'd lost a pet once; it was something no kid should go through. Plus, Heather really was the closest person to a friend Eric had in this new place, so it seemed like the right thing to do. Without looking away from the flier, Eric responded.

"I will, mom. For sure."

His mom smiled with pride. Her son could be a little strange and he had a nasty habit of only telling half the story, but he was a good person.

"If you want to stay out all day, I can make you some snacks to take with you."

Eric thanked his mom and then grabbed himself a bowl of cereal. Two bowls. He was going to need some serious energy if he was going to help Heather look for poor old Hoss. After putting down breakfast in record time, Eric got cleaned up and dressed and walked over to Heather's house. Mrs. Foster answered the door, a rather tired and weary look on her face, almost too tired to prevent her nasty cigarette from falling from her mouth.

"Hey, Eric. Little early isn't it?"

"Sorry, Mrs. Foster. I just. Well, mom showed me this flier about Hoss and I wanted to help."

Mrs. Foster took the paper from his hands. She did not look happy.

"Dang that girl, she thinks printer ink just grows on trees and can..." Eric flinched at the next string of words that came from Mrs. Foster's mouth. "Oh, sorry, Eric. I sometimes forget my manners around you kids. Stupid girl. A reward! As if we have the money to even feed that living vacuum of a dog, let alone offer a reward if we find him."

Eric looked a little surprised.

"So you aren't looking for Hoss?"

Mrs. Foster handed the now crumpled and slightly stinky bit of paper back to him.

"My daughter is looking for him and she apparently thinks I'm gonna pay someone if they find that annoying beast. Dang her." With that, Mrs. Foster flung her cigarette from her hands, so close that Eric did a quick head slide to the left in order to avoid any random bit of cancerous glowing embers from landing in his hair.

Mrs. Foster shouted back into her house.

"Heather Jenna Marie Lynn Foster, you get your butt out here now!"

Eric took a reflexive step back at the mention of his friend's full name. All kids knew that when a parent yelled your full name, you were in serious trouble. He then chuckled a bit to himself when he thought about just how many names Heather had. Thankfully Mrs. Foster's own screaming drowned out his chuckle, as it would have surely been met with scorn. Mrs. Foster yelled louder still when her daughter did not emerge from her bedroom. So loud was the yell that his own mother popped her head outside Eric's front door. Eric looked back and shrugged. His mom took that as a sign that things were relatively okay and went back inside. Mrs. Foster, growing angrier still, turned to Eric. "Well, come in. I'll rouse her highness from bed. Summer or not, she ain't gonna sleep the day away."

She kept speaking to no one as she walked down the hall. "If she thinks she can promise a reward and expect to not lift a finger, she's got another..." Mrs. Foster again stopped her rant in mid-sentence with a series of words that Eric had never even heard his dad say after slamming his hand in the car door once. These were some seriously juicy and colorful terms. A moment later, Mrs. Foster emerged from Heather's room with yet another note.

"Stupid kid is out there somewhere, looking for that dumb dog." She handed the note to a very confused Eric and lit up another cigarette. Eric did his best to stifle a cough, but was not successful.

"Sorry, I forgot Heather told me. You and your weak set of lungs. Anyway, looks like you might as well go. If you run into that idiotic daughter of mine, you tell her to get her butt back home. She and I are going to have some words."

Eric looked at the note.

"Mom. Got up early. Went looking for Hoss. Sorry about the kitchen."

Eric tried to lean his head in the direction of the kitchen, but Mrs. Foster stood in his view. Eric just put the note in his pocket and looked back at Mrs. Foster.

"Um, my mom made us snacks. I mean, we can stay out all day."

Mrs. Foster waved him off.

"Whatever. Just tell her the longer she's out, the more trouble she's in."

Eric nodded.

"Um. Okay." With that, he left his friend's house, wondering just where she had gone and what he would tell her when he found her.

Although Ashen Forest Estates was by no means a massive neighborhood, it was still large enough that simply walking around the area would do little in helping Eric to find his friend. So, with the morning sun just a few hours over the horizon and a backpack of snacks securely attached, Eric got on his bike and pedaled down the road. "Maybe I'll ride past Lazer's house last, um, after I find Heather," he said out loud, thankful that no one could hear his rather timid inner monolog. It bothered Eric a bit that it took a missing friend to get him to explore the place he was likely going to call home for a very long time, at least until high school, and to someone just a few months past his eleventh birthday, that was an eternity indeed. Only a few minutes into his quest and Eric was slowly learning that Ashen Forest Estates was a study in contradiction. On any given street he would see a massive home with yards so meticulously maintained that even his mom would think they'd gone too far, only to see a home next to it that was barely standing on the cement cinder blocks that were never meant as a long term solution for a foundation. Perfect lawns and flower gardens gave way to unchecked wilderness or levels of junk hoarding that were simply screaming for a reality television crew to arrive. One thing that almost every house shared was a vibe that suggested you weren't welcome unless specifically invited. Yards that lacked a tall and locked fence were instead peppered with No Trespassing signs, or the ever colorful Never Mind the Dog, Beware the Human signs, often hammered into a tree that did not ask for such treatment. But still, Eric pressed on, every few minutes yelling Heather's name and pausing, hoping he would hear her rather strong voice yell back. For close to thirty minutes, Eric heard nothing.

Turning up the hill, he rode into the less populated area of Ashen Estates. "If ever a map needed to read 'Here there be monsters,' it'd be for this place." Not caring that he was speaking to himself, Eric slowed his pace a bit on his bike. The homes got a little older, with more than a few looking more like extensions of an angry tree than a real house. For reasons he didn't fully understand, Eric stopped his bike, set it on the kickstand, and looked for some kind of weapon. It wasn't that he thought he could knock back whatever was waiting for him in this rather foreboding area of Ashen Estates. But he at least wanted to be able to tell his dad, as his mom tended another injury, that he put up an effort to defend himself. He bent down and grabbed a stick that looked more like a broken tree limb that was about half the size of his body. "Yeah, this should work," he again said out loud. Were anyone else with Eric at the time, they would have told him that perhaps grabbing a chunk of wood so large he couldn't swing it with any force was a bad idea. Alas, there was no such person, and Eric got back on his bike and did his best to move forward while balancing his "weapon." The incline grew as he rode deeper into the neighborhood. It was an incline that would not have been an issue at all for someone like Heather, who seemed to be made of nothing but skinny muscles and freckles. But to someone like Eric, who was far more comfortable on the floor with a book, it was a ride of marathon-like proportions. He didn't even have the time to catch his breath at the top of the hill when he saw that fire-headed horror known as Rusty tossing Heather's fliers into the air as Rusty's little toad of a henchman poked at her. For a moment Eric thought about doing nothing. There was a part of him that really felt like Heather could mop up both these guys. But he also remembered how he felt the day he learned his pet was never coming home. The pain in his heart. The weakness that made everything a massive task. At that moment Eric decided it was time to pay back his friend for saving him from a rampaging dog. He just hoped he would survive the attempt.

From the top of the hill, Eric looked down at his new friend, doing her best to contain her emotions as Rusty ripped apart the remaining posters for her missing dog and flung the bits into the air. Although it was a relatively calm day, the usual slight breeze in Ashen Estates took her posters into yards, ditches, and burn piles. There was no salvaging them. Rusty and his friend seemed content to simply laugh at her growing anger. Eric steadied himself and raised his wooden weapon into the air. Reaching deep within his own memory of epic one-liners destined to strike both fear and awe in his enemies, Eric shouted to those below him.

"Unhand her, you fiends!"

Even as he heard the words leave his mouth, Eric, the boy that loved all things fantasy, knew he'd uttered what was quite possibly the worst battle cry in the history of battle cries. Rusty and his sidekick turned to face Eric, taking their time to see who dared interrupt their time-tested bullying tactics. Seeing it was the small new kid that had already been dropped by one fast gut punch, their laughter echoed throughout all corners of Ashen Estates. And even though he was there to help her, Eric couldn't help but notice the utter shock on

Heather's face. He just wished he'd said anything other than "Unhand her, you fiends."

Rusty told his sidekick, whom he simply called Spit, to stay with Heather as he made the slow and deliberate walk towards Eric.

"And just what do you think you're going to do to us... What did you call me? Friend?"

Eric did his best to hold his place on the ground.

"No. I said fiend. And if you spent more time reading papers instead of ripping them apart, you might know what that means." His mom was right; there was going to be a time when not only would his mouth not get him out of trouble, it would actively get him in deeper. It looked like that time had finally come.

Rusty's face contorted in anger. Eric could tell Rusty was getting ready for a full-speed charge at him. Eric moved to get off the bike, holding his branch like a club, and then something in him snapped. Eric squinted his eyes. Time seemed to slow down all around him. Eric's choice felt clear as he sat back on the seat of his bike. Rusty was shouting all manner of vulgar taunts and ways in which he would inflict pain upon Eric once he got to the top of the hill. Eric processed none of it. He sat up tall and true on his secondhand BMX bike. He braced the large branch under his right arm. And then, with more power than sense, Eric pedaled his bike harder than he ever had before. All around him the setting shifted from one of Ashen Forest Estates and into an epic dual between mounted knight and beast. Even if Rusty knew what was coming, he had no time to react.

With speed and power that even shocked Eric, his branch

slammed into Rusty's right shoulder. The impact sent both Eric and his foe flying into the air. Rusty let out a wail of pain that reminded Eric that, for all the boy's taunting and physical presence, he was still a kid. And kids screamed when they got hurt. And these were all thoughts Eric would process later, if he survived the next few moments. His bike again went out from under him as he hit the pavement hard. He barely kept his head from slamming down, with his hands taking the bulk of the impact and rough dragging. Rusty was still laying on the ground a few feet away, yelling in both pain and anger. Heather took the moment and threw her surprisingly powerful frame into Spit. Clearly inheriting her mother's rather colorful verbal skills, poor Spit was no match for Heather as she unloaded on the boy who was obviously more confident when he had someone big to stand behind.

Leaving Spit to lick his own wounds, Heather helped Eric up. She smiled at him, her face a mixture of fear, relief, and no small amount of tears. To his credit, somehow Eric kept it all together, be it from a sense of pride or just the fact that he was still slightly living in his own fantasy of the knight saving the princess. As Heather thanked him she put an end to his rather outdated fantasy.

"I guess we're even now. Come on, let's get out of here before those two get it together."

Eric nodded.

"Sounds good to me. Then we can get back to looking for your dog."

Heather actually teared up a bit more at Eric's one-track mind.

"I'm really happy for your help and I think we're gonna be

good friends, but let's just get home first." She glanced back at her own bike, sitting on the ground where Spit continued to cry. "No way we go back for that. Sorry, Eric, but you're on the back. I'm getting us out of here."

Without a word of protest, Eric let Heather take control of his bike as he held onto her for the ride back. To any regular boy, letting a girl, even an older one, pedal your bike home would be a grave insult to his budding ego. Eric, however, understood that ego didn't matter if you weren't able to perform a tactical retreat. And their was no getting around it; Heather was just stronger than him. Ego was for another time. They needed to get away. Eric held on tight as Heather's legs removed them from the violent scene as fast as she could pedal. Which, to Eric's surprise, was quite fast. Not enjoying the silence, Eric starting talking as Heather got them home.

"I went to your house this morning. You're mom is really mad."

Heather didn't answer immediately as she pedaled them both away from this dangerous area of Ashen Forest Estates.

"Yeah, about that. Mind if we go to your house for a while"?

Eric didn't pause one bit.

"Sounds like a great plan. Although we better think of a real good story to tell my mom."

He could almost hear Heather's smile.

"That's easy. We'll tell her you got hurt saving me this time. All moms like a hero."

Eric was taken aback.

"Hero?"

Heather slightly turned her head as she made the corner

and got within eyesight of Eric's house.

"Don't let it go to your head, shorty. But for now. Yes, Eric Del Bosque, you're my hero".

Even though he could hear the almost cartoon-like sarcasm in Heather's voice, Eric smiled all the way home.

10
SOME EXPLAINING TO DO

"Shoot, this is one of my favorite shirts," proclaimed Heather. Eric took his grip off her shoulders and stepped off the back of his bike. Unsure what she was talking about, Eric raised an eyebrow.

"What? Get a bunch of dirt on it?"

Heather set the bike down, blatantly ignoring the kickstand and Eric's annoyed grimace as his bike hit the dirt. "Dirt washes off. But the blood stains left by your messed up hands will not."

Eric looked down at his hands. She wasn't kidding. Both the top of his hands and his palms were a rather nasty collection of ruddy red and brown wounds with little patches of Ashen Forest Estates dirt and asphalt nuggets. He was more than a little shocked that they didn't sting more. "Oh, um, sorry about that. We can ask my mom to wash your shirt."

Heather shrugged and stared down at herself. "Eh, I was probably going to grow out of it soon enough anyway." Eric still looked a little confused. Heather rolled her eyes and smiled. "You really are a strange guy, Eric. Even in your cluelessness, you're rather hilarious."

Eric smiled back. "Thanks, I think."

Heather waved her arms toward the door.

"I do believe the promise of food was made." Eric nodded and took the still temporary, but looking more permanent with each passing day, construction steps into his house. The pain notwithstanding, he was feeling pretty good about himself. That was all about to change when he rounded the corner into his living room and came face to face with his mother.

"One hour. You were gone one hour and this is how you come back! One. Hour. I can't believe—" His mom stopped her rant long enough to see that Heather was actually in far worse shape than he was. Eric was so wrapped up in the actions of helping his friend and their speedy get away, he never thought to ask how she was feeling. It was only then that he noticed that his friend had dried blood around her mouth and what looked like the beginning of a world class black eye.

"Oh, my sweet Lord. Heather! What happened? Oh, sweet thing. Oh. Please, sit down. Sit. Eric. Eric! Stop gawking and get my medical kit. Hurry, I might be able to keep the swelling down. Then we're calling you mom."

Heather made an early attempt at protest at the prospect of calling her own mother. It was no use. The whirlwind of overprotection that was Eric's mom was in full swing. Eric didn't even pause to say "Okay," instead making an immediate beeline to his parents' bathroom and his mom's legendary medical kit.

Most households had some form of first aid kit, the basics, like a simple collection of bandages and maybe a bit of rubbing alcohol. Such was not the case in the Del Bosque household. Eric's mom took her medical treatment seriously and unless blood was actually gushing from a wound or a bit of bone was sticking out of you, she was keeping you out of the hospital. Not because she had any fear or disdain for those in the medical profession. Far from it. She loved it. And after taking years of courses and workshops on basic and advanced first aid, Eric was fairly sure he trusted his own mom over someone he never met. He rushed into his parents' bathroom and flung open the cabinet that contained the massive metal box. It really was a disservice to call it a first aid kit. He'd taken tours of fire and police stations in the past and this large blue metal box rivaled what most of those places stored. Indeed he was all but certain only an ambulance had more on-the-scene medical gear. In fact, Eric was sure his mom had a few things in this metal container that would earn her some probing questions from local authorities. He had no idea how she got some of these items, and like so many things, Eric decided he didn't want to know.

Eric grunted under the weight of the metal box as his mom yelled for him to stop messing around. The case was a pain to carry when his muscles weren't aching. The pain had been masked by an adrenaline rush that was starting to subside. "I'm coming," was the best he could muster as he made his way back.

Just as he dropped the medical kit on the counter he heard his mom reply, "Well, don't tell me, just—oh, good." Earlina flung the box open and began digging into its very well organized, but still dense contents.

Heather looked as if she were about to protest all this attention at her physical condition, a condition she seemed more than capable of dealing with. Eric merely looked at her, placed his own finger to his lips in the universal "shushing" manner, and slowly shook his head. His eyes told Heather all she needed to know. Straining as if telepathy were real, Eric leaned towards his friend and thought, "Don't even try. It's not worth it. You're going to get fixed whether you like it or not."

Heather understood such non-verbal concepts and leaned back on the couch. She awaited her medical aid.

Earlina returned to Heather with all manner of swabs, liquids, and creams. Each one looked like it was going to hurt more than the actual event that caused her injuries. Heather cringed as Eric's mom started cleaning her nose.

"Sorry, sweetie. Well, good news is, it isn't broken."

Heather looked up at the woman she barely knew who was now providing her with more medical attention than her own mother had in her thirteen years on this planet.

"Ho can youf tell?" mumbled Heather as Eric tried not to giggle as his mom's continued actions caused Heather to sound like she was nursing a week-long cold.

"Honestly? You'd be screaming bloody murder if I'd touched your nose and it was broken. Sorry." Heather's eyes widened at that thought and then smiled. "I wasn't joking," Eric's mom replied. Heather stopped smiling. She was beginning to understand. While Earlina was one of the nicer adults she had met, this woman was all business when it came to taking care of the injured. Although motherly instincts were in play, it was rather obvious that Eric's mother took pride and enjoyment from this form of medical triage. Eric looked at Heather and nodded back. Again, their minds seem to share the same thought: "See what I mean." They both sheepishly smiled at each other. Eric's mom, still in all business mode, got out the creams and almost medieval-looking wooden application sticks.

"Now, before the two of you keep making googly eyes at each other and are able to sync up a story to tell me, start speaking. One of you. Now."

Both Eric and Heather looked shocked. Eric only nodded and mouthed to his friend. "Leave it. To. Me." Heather, knowing how she could play her part, started to talk and then let out a wholly believable cry of pain and leaned back.

Earlina genuinely felt bad and turned to her son.

"Okay, just you explain. What the heck were you two doing that in one hour you were able to cause this much damage?"

Eric's brain went into creative overdrive. This one was going to be tricky. He didn't want to lie to his mom, but he also didn't need her going all neighborhood crusader. Not yet at least.

"When I went over to Mrs. Foster's house, like you saw, she told me that Heather had gone out already to look for her dog. So I went to the spot where I figured she would start looking first."

Seeing that his mother was already sensing some deception in her son's opening statement, Heather added in a weak voice,

"I told Eric that Hoss, my dog, he likes to play by the pond at the north end of the neighborhood." Then, to really sell it, she let a little tear slide down the side of her face. Eric couldn't tell if it was the pain, the fact that her dog was still missing, or a combination of the both but he was impressed none the less by her help. Earlina merely nodded and told Eric to continue.

"Right, so I rode to the pond and I saw Heather at the edge of the pond. She must have hit a rock or something because she was lying in the dirt and holding her. Um..." Heather blinked her eyes quickly, acting as if something was making them sting, just as Eric's mom turned back toward the medical kit to grab some more gauze and tape. Eric recovered quickly. "Her eye. I guess she smacked it when her bike went over."

Earlina was honestly concerned.

"Your poor thing. You need to wear a helmet, young lady. And you," she added as she applied the gauze, "I better never see you without yours."

Eric nodded. There was no way he was going to argue that one. "I know mom." He continued,

"Anyway, I was in such a hurry to get down there and help her that I wasn't paying attention. My shoelaces came untied and—"

Again, Eric's mom cut him off with just a bit of desperate annoyance. "How many times have I told you to double lace those things when you go out?"

Eric kept up the appearance of apology. "I know. I know. I'm sorry."

His mom returned her attention to Heather, who seemed to be more uncomfortable by the increasing attention to her safety than the actual injuries to herself. "So, let me guess. Your laces got in the chain?"

Eric smiled at his mom.

"Yeah, sorry. But I'm okay."

His mom gave Heather an intense once-over and declared her fit to stand, if she had the energy. Heather stood up, steadied herself on the arm of the couch a bit and smiled at Eric's mom.

"Thanks, Mrs. Del Bosque. I didn't think it looked that bad."

Without a moment's hestitation, Eric and his mother replied in unison.

"Small things can kill you—my grandma once..."

Earlina cut her son off.

"That's not funny, Eric. I'm serious."

Eric smiled.

"I know, mom. But you say it every time."

Even his mom couldn't contain her grin.

"Okay, smart guy, your turn." And with that she gestured for Eric to sit on the couch. He again knew there was no point in resisting. As she started to work on her son, Earlina's face tightened up a bit. Eric felt a twinge of concern within himself. He knew that meant one thing and one thing only—that his mom had been slowly milling about his story and was starting to see some cracks in it. That was the danger with everyone knowing you had a massively active imagination. Half of what came out of your mouth was already assumed to be just a bit on the exaggerated side.

Taking a swab of hydrogen peroxide, Earlina rather roughly started to clean the wounds on both the tops and bottoms of Eric's hands.

"I thought you said you were near a pond?"

Eric murmured a basic "Uh-huh," and hoped she didn't pry more. The fuzzing liquid on his hands stung like crazy and it made it harder to keep up a story.

His mom wasn't backing down. "Then why am I pulling little bits of road from your hands?"

This time is was Heather who stepped in with the quick thinking. They really were in this one together.

"Well, Mrs. Del Bosque. When I say 'pond,' that's just what the kids call it. It's really just a gravel pit the road crew uses to repair the roads. It doesn't have much water now, but it's usually filled with water in the early spring and late fall, so we just call it the pond."

Earlina sat still for a moment, wondering if these two were being completely honest or if her son now had a friend that was just as sneaky as he. For now, she was content to give them both the benefit of the doubt.

"Okay. Well, no more biking for the both of you. Heather, are you sure you shouldn't tell your mom you're okay?"

Heather moved to the window and looked across the street. Her mom's one working car wasn't in the driveway.

"It's okay. Besides, I can tell she isn't home right now. She must have gone into town. Or, something." There was a sadness in her voice that both Eric and his mom caught. Eric went to say something, but his mom gently shook her head to wave him off. He understood and didn't pry.

"Well, then, I am going to make you two some lunch and you are more than welcome to hang out here."

Heather's gloom subsided. "Thanks, Mrs. Del Bosque."

She didn't let Heather finish. "Please, call me Earlina. Mrs. Del Bosque is what the bag boy calls me; I'll not have

Eric's friend doing the same."

Heather smiled, "Okay, Earlina."

Eric was happy that they'd made it past his mom's rather sharp prying mind, but a part of him was a little nervous at the almost instant familiarity Heather and his mom were sharing. Without thinking, he jumped in.

"Hey, mom, can I show Heather my room?"

Earlina nodded and he waved at Heather to follow him. Eric's mom chimed down at them,

"Leave the door open!" Eric turned, and with a confused look, asked why. His mom replied, "Don't worry about why," a phrase with an implied tone that also said, "And don't push it, boy."

Eric shrugged and said, "Fine," oblivious to Heather's slight blush and his mom's small grin. He was, as was often the case, completely oblivious to all but the most obvious events around him.

"You've been living up here for almost three weeks and you still haven't unpacked your room all the way."

Eric shrugged as he got on his hands and knees and reached under his bed. The bed muffled his reply. "Ha, ha." Heather looked for a place to sit, seeing a trunk labeled Action figures, she plopped down and waited to see what Eric was doing. Eric got up from the floor, holding a very old-looking book. His look was one of complete seriousness.

"I think I might have an idea about what happened to your dog."

Heather looked at the book in his hands. The title read The Tale of Tocho.

Heather looked confused. Eric cracked the book open. "Just

listen to this."

11
A DAY OF RESEARCH

Eric and Heather spent more than a couple of hours going over what Eric had read in The Tale of Tocho. Even though Eric sounded a little crazy as he connected the events in what looked like a fictional story about a young Native American girl and Heather's missing dog, he was making a pretty strong case.

"Look, I know there hasn't been a volcanic eruption in over a hundred years, but I don't really think whatever is out there needs the volcano anymore."

Heather tilted her head.

"I don't think anyone ever really needs a volcano, Eric." He could tell she was humoring him, but believing very little of what was coming from his mouth.

"I know that. Listen, when I went to the library yesterday, Mr. Gregory said some strange things to me."

Heather again countered, "That's because Mr. Gregory is a strange guy. Everyone knows that."

Eric shook his head. "You don't understand. I know he's a

little weird, but this was different. At first he was just the normal wild-haired guy all the kids make jokes about. But when I asked for information about the year of the eruption he got—well, he got weirder. Even a little spooky."

Although Heather still seemed wholly unimpressed by Eric's passionate explanations, she leaned in closer to hear what he was going on about. Eric waved at Heather to come sit closer to him, as if being within proximity to the book he was holding was exerting a greater influence on her opinion. "This book right here—it's the only item I can find that actually talks about the time period during the Mount Ashen eruption. And I am pretty sure this is the only copy to exist."

Heather raised an eyebrow.

"Then how did you get a hold of it?" Her eyes widened. "Oh, did you steal it?" Eric shot at her a look that bordered on genuine hurt. Heather raised her hands and said, "Whoa, sorry. It wasn't like I'd asked if you just kicked a kitten." Eric did not find this concept humorous at all.

"Calm down, shorty, I was only kidding. Well, maybe a little. But, your reaction is duly noted."

Eric leaned back into the book, shaking off the joke.

"I don't think this is just some fictional story about this girl named Tocho. I think these events actually happened. I think someone wrote down everything in this book."

Heather leaned in closer. Whatever he was about to say was clearly important because Eric started to lower his voice.

"Just hear me out. I think you and I are were meant to know about this book. I think we're supposed to finish what Tocho started."

Heather had heard enough. Although not angry, she wasn't going to allow herself to be pulled into the wild ravings of a boy that hadn't even started junior high school.

"Really, Eric? I'm starting to think your mom is right. You do spend way too much time in your own head. You think my missing dog, the strange sounds outside at night, the recent quake, and this boring book about some Native American girl is all part of one massive adventure where you and I become animal-possessing monster hunters!"

Eric dropped the book on his bed.

"No, not hunters. Were you even listening to me?"

Heather's voice started to shake as she replied.

"Yes, I was. What I want to know is if you were listening to yourself. Listen to how crazy it all sounds. You want to help me find my dog. Thank you. Yes, please. I would really like that. But all this other stuff? It's just crap, all of it. I just want my dog back!"

Eric could tell he had missed the whole point of the afternoon. For a moment, lost in his own wild ideas of grand adventure, he forgot the whole reason why he knocked on Heather's door this morning. Why he charged down the hill like a jousting knight into the neighborhood bully. He looked at his friend as tears started to well in her eyes and felt his own eyes welling up. "I'm sorry. I guess I do let myself get carried away. Let's go back out. Let's go look for your dog."

Heather wiped away her tears. It was strange for Eric to see her that way. Sure, they'd only known each other for a few weeks, but in that time, Heather seemed so much bigger and stronger than him. Not just in the physical sense, which was all too obvious, but in her character. Everything was a laugh to her. Even her mom, running out at any hour of the day or night. She faced it all with a grin. This morning, as Rusty and Spit were throwing her posters to the wind and breaking her bike, she never once lost her cool. But now, sitting on Eric's bed as he did his best to convince her that this book and her missing dog were all connected, Eric saw something else. In the short time they'd been friends, he saw someone that didn't care that he was this small bookish kid, and that he didn't care that she was a gangly girl that lived in a junkyard. She believed in him. The least he could do was the same for her. His stories, even if they were true or not, could wait for a better day. Today, he had to help his friend find her beloved pet.

"Come on, let's ask my mom to drive us back to your bike. Even if Rusty is still around, he's not going to mess with us with an adult around."

Heather nodded at him, a redness still in her eyes. "Sounds like a good plan."

He stood up and held out his hand, and with a smile, reached to hers. "We'll find him."

She nodded back.

"And, Eric, I'm sorry I put the whole idea of Hairy Baby in your head. I mean, us kids always joke about it, but none of us has ever really seen it. I mean, not really."

Eric's grin slowly faded from his face, as if some realization was creeping into his mind. He gently let go of Heather's hand and reached back to the book. Their minor friends' tiff over, Heather rolled her eyes and waited to see what Eric was doing this time.

He opened the book and flipped through it again, skimming

quickly till he got to near the end of the book. "How long have people talked about this Hairy Baby?"

Heather shoved her hands in her pockets. She was a little annoyed, but Eric's obsession was her fault, even just a bit, so she played along.

"My mom remembers kids talking about it since she was in the first grade, and if the older kids were talking about it then, since before TV, I guess."

Eric's eyes grew wide.

"Wow, that's a long time."

Heather agreed. "I know."

Eric slowed his skimming a bit. "Hairy Baby, no. No. No. Hairy. Harree, nope. Wait." Eric revealed a massive smile that looked like someone had just gotten away with the best crime of all time. He turned the book over so Heather could see what he was looking at.

She leaned in. "I don't see it."

Eric pointed at the page. "Right here. Tocho mentions a legend brought to life after the eruption. Here. She calls it the 'Hemei Ninambebea.'"

Heather again shrugged. "Great; what does that have to do with you and I finding my dog again?"

Eric turned the book back so he could read it aloud. "'The Hemei Ninambebea has only been a story told by my elders since my own grandmother was a child. But they speak of a time when the grounds will open and the darkest of these spirits will be set free to control the beasts that walk the lands. And then, the Hemei Ninambebea will feast upon those that can not cast it back.'" Eric shut the book and looked at Heather. Although she still wasn't sure, Eric could see a small part of her was starting to connect the dots. For better or worse, she was starting to believe him.

Eric kept talking as he set the book down.

"I think there is something strange buried in this town and our neighborhood is just part of that strangeness. I think everyone tried to wipe out what happened here the year the volcano erupted and the ground tore open. I think maybe the adults have kept the secrets of Grizzlydale buried for so long, they've forgotten. I think what they forgot is starting to claw its way back out."

Heather stopped him, "And you think my missing dog has something to do with all of this?"

Eric nodded a little.

"I think if we find him, we might be closer to finding out and maybe even stopping whatever happened in this book."

Heather let out a deep breath. "Okay, Eric. I'll play along. For now. But we really need to find my little buddy. Please."

Eric nodded with a grim determination his friend had never seen.

"Tonight, we go out and find him. I promise."

12
THE DINNER TALK

Eric was glad he had asked his mom to take him and Heather back to the spot where she left her bike behind. Well, "left behind" was using the term loosely, as neither wanted to divulge the real reason why Heather's bike was still at the scene. When his mom pulled up, Eric's suspicions proved correct when he saw both Rusty and his worm of a sidekick, Spit, waiting around Heather's bike. Both pairs of kids seemed unwilling to reveal to the lone adult as to why they were all there. It was code that both hero and villain would follow until escalation, and Eric was concerned there would indeed be escalation, an escalation that would force a parental hand.

Thankfully, his mom didn't press at all when she saw a few more kids. Partially correct in her assumption that this was a popular place to play and ride bikes, she chalked it up to coincidence. Her steady gaze upon both her son and Heather prevented Rusty and Spit from even making a threatening stance as they picked up her bike, which was far worse for wear than they'd left it when they pedaled for home. As

Heather picked up the bike to place it into Earlina's car, the chain and a few random bits fell to the ground. Neither Rusty nor Spit moved to pick them up. Instead, they quietly threatened both kids as Eric grabbed the small pieces. Upon returning, Earlina asked what those boys said, both Eric and Heather gave the non-committal reply of "Nothing." This seemed a fine enough answer for the time being.

The ride back to Eric's house was short and silent. Both Eric and his mom seemed to understand that Heather was in for a rough afternoon when her mom came home from wherever she went and saw her bike. Eric thought about asking his mom if Heather could stay for dinner. But a part of him knew that even if she wanted to say yes, which she probably would have, Heather wouldn't be able to accept.

Fair or not, Eric understood that Heather was going to have to take whatever was waiting for her. He looked at his friend and smiled; she returned the smile, both understanding what the other was thinking. Although his age of eleven and hers of thirteen made them seem years apart in the grand child hierarchy, both understood what was going to happen when she got home. And both were bothered by the fact that the other friend couldn't do anything about it.

Earlina pulled into the driveway of their house and helped Heather unload the heavily damaged bike. His mom patted Heather on the back. "It's not so bad, sweetie. Besides, you're safe. Your mom will be grateful for that."

Heather thanked Earlina as she carried her bike and made her way back. Eric jumped from the car, "Wait! You forgot these." Both Earlina and Heather turned to see what Eric was talking about. From his pocket Eric produced a tattered roll of gauze, some medical tape, and a sample packet of antibiotic cream. Earlina smiled at the apparent thoughtfulness of her son. Heather smiled as she saw her friend nod and wink at her. She nodded to Earlina and turned back to her house. On her way home, Heather looked down at the various first aid items Eric gave her. Badly written on the tape was the sentence: "Tonight we'll start the search." She couldn't help but chuckle quietly to herself. There wasn't a stranger or more eager person in her life than Eric and she wouldn't have it any other way. Before heading into her house, Heather turned around again. "Thanks again! I'll make sure!"

Earlina waved back.

"What did she mean by that?"

Eric grinned.

"I told her to get better, so we can keep looking for her dog."

Earlina replied with a knowing, "Ah," and tilted her head toward the house. "Well, inside. Your dad is pulling another double, so it's just you and me for dinner. Hot dogs and tortillas?"

Eric broke into a full toothed grin.

"Can I grill them?"

Earlina laughed.

"You bet."

The two of them went inside and prepared the rather bizarre dinner that only they could appreciate. And while Eric normally focused all his attention on the fine art of hot dog grilling, his mind was decidedly elsewhere as he wondered just what kind of adventures he and Heather would find when the sun went down tonight.

"You oaf'kay son?" asked his mom, talking, quite against character, with her mouth full of charred hotdog and warm flour tortilla. Eric realized he was starring into nothingness when his mom's garbled question brought him back to the moment. Still not fully sure what she asked, Eric gave the universal look for "what" to his mom.

"I said," she continued before putting her finger up to show she needed a moment. Then, after a second, she continued. "I said, are you okay? I mean, it's not very often we get to have this for dinner and even less when I let us eat while sitting on the couch watching TV."

Eric shook himself completely. There was no way he was going to tell his mom the reason he was lost in thought. Of what he and Heather would find when they headed out into the great dark unknown that was Ashen Forest Estates once the sun set. Instead, he spoke yet another half truth that was sadly becoming the norm between them.

"Oh, no. Sorry, mom. No, this is really great. I just... I guess I'm still a little tired from today." He felt bad for not telling her the real reason for his distraction. But he also knew she would not only forbid the two of them from heading out, but she would likely stay up all night to make sure Eric knew she wasn't messing around. Without thinking, Eric continued. "I guess I'm just worried about Heather as well."

Saying the words out loud, even Eric was caught off guard by his feelings, now made real by his own voice. His mom pressed the issue.

"What do you mean, mijo?"

There was no sense in retracting his comment now. And to be honest, Eric genuinely was worried about his friend. They hadn't known each other very long, but Heather was someone he enjoyed being around. His whole life, Eric had known a lot of kids, but none of them ever considered him a friend. It was nice. Nice, and a little confusing.

"Well, I just worry that her mom is going to be really mad at her. And when I went over there, Mrs. Foster didn't seem like she cared about Heather. I mean, I know she does because she's her mom, but. I don't know, she only yells at her. And not when she's in trouble. I mean all the time. All she does is yell."

Earlina smiled at her son and set her plate on the TV tray. This wasn't going to be an easy conversation.

"I know we don't have a lot, Eric, but what we do have is each other, your father and I. And I'm not saying anyone is better or worse for that. But, when only one person has to run everything, when one person has to make all the money, well, that's really hard, and sometimes when you work that hard you get tired. Very tired. So tired that even the simplest of tasks takes all your energy, and unfortunately, sometimes all some people have left is anger." Eric looked at his mom; part of what she was saying made sense. "And you are right; Mrs. Foster does love her daughter. But sometimes when you're that tired and you work that hard, everything makes you snap. Like how you and I have to be extra quiet when your dad pulls a double?" Eric nodded at that; that he understood all too well. "Imagine every day being like that. And it sounds like that's the case with Mrs. Foster. She's always that tired."

Eric was starting to see what his mom meant. He took another bite of his far from fancy, but so very tasty dinner.

THE DINNER TALK

"What if we offered to help? I mean, what if we told Mrs. Foster that Heather could stay with us some of the time. I mean, we could. Couldn't we?"

Eric's mom leaned forward and shook her head.

"No. We can't". Eric looked confused. "Eric, your heart is in the right place. You're a very kind person and for that, I will always be proud." Earlina could tell Eric still wasn't quite understanding where she was going with all this. "But sometimes you have to let people work through things on their own. Sometimes helping them only makes them feel even worse. Does that make any sense?" Eric shook his head. "Okay. Let me think." She took another bite and leaned back on the couch. "Okay, imagine this. Say you've spent all this time on one of your stories. You work day and night on making it the best story you can. But, no matter how hard you work, it just doesn't seem right. You just can't make it work. Still, you know that what you are doing is the best you can do at the time and even though it isn't what you want, you're still very proud of it."

Eric leaned forward, taking in all that his mom had to say. "Now, you've done all that and then, all of a sudden, someone shows up, even someone you really like, and tells you they can fix all the mistakes you made. That they can make your story better if you just stop working on it. How would that make you feel?"

Eric knew exactly what his mom was going for and didn't hesitate with his answer.

"Pretty annoyed. Maybe even a little hurt."

Earlina smiled.

"And that's why we can't ask Mrs. Foster to take care of

Heather, even for a couple days." While Eric understood, he was still clearly bothered that he couldn't do more to help his friend. Sensing the conflict in her son, Earlina added one more thing. "Now, if Mrs. Foster ever asks if we can help out because of work, or school, then yes, of course we can and we'll be happy to."

Eric smiled. It wasn't much, but it was enough to make him feel a little better. He went back to his dinner, which had grown cold, and almost instantly his thoughts returned to pending adventures. While it was still a little early, Eric knew he needed to get some rest if he was going to be of any use tonight.

Eric got up and took his plate into the kitchen. From the living room, his mom cut him off. "Hey, don't just leave it on the counter. Come on now; put it in the dishwasher." Eric did so without a word of rebuttal. It wasn't worth the hassle and he was just grateful that hot dogs and tortillas really had no form of clean up. Walking out of the kitchen he turned to his mom.

"I'm pretty tired and a little sore still from today. Do you mind if I go to bed early?"

Any other mother would find such behavior odd. However, Earlina long ago learned her son was anything but normal, and when he said he wanted to go to bed early, he really meant it. Well, what he really meant was that he would read for hours on end and then finally pass out with a book in his hands.

She smiled and told him it was fine. As he leaned in to hug his mom goodnight, she asked, "Do you want to grab a book from the chest? I know you haven't spent that much time outside the past few days. But, the time that you did was a little dramatic, so I think you've earned a book or two."

Eric stepped back and shook his head.

"Naw, I'm okay, mom." Almost immediately, he knew that he'd made a mistake. No matter how tired, he would have never turned down a chance to dig into the chest of books. His mom arched an eyebrow in genuine questioning. Eric had to think fast lest she ask what was really bothering him.

"Wait. No. I mean yes. I would. Sorry, I'm guess I'm still thinking about what you said about Heather and her mom. Yes. Please, I want to grab something new."

His mom looked at him for a moment. Eric wasn't sure if she was going to press the matter. He held still as she looked at him some more.

"That's more like it."

Eric let out a small sigh as she motioned for him to select something. She said, "It's not locked, but don't get any ideas. I've counted."

Eric wasn't sure if that part was true or not, but he figured it was best to not push his mom on that front. He spent just enough time to allow his mom to think he was really thinking about what book to grab, though in truth he just took what was on top. He made his way back to his room and held the single book in the air.

"Just one, I promise." He couldn't see his mom grinning to herself as he made his way to his room.

Eric dropped the book on his recently cleared-up desk and

proceeded to open The Tale of Tocho. This was the only book he needed to go over tonight. Glancing at his clock he saw that he still had a few hours before it was time. Before he and Heather set out on their first quest. Adventure was indeed afoot.

13
THE NIGHT HUNT

Eric made sure he completed his nightly ritual of saying goodnight to his mom, even though he'd gone to his room a few hours before. Popping out for just a few seconds to give the nightly greeting was the only way he could be sure she wouldn't check in on him to see if he was asleep. Or, as was often the case, burning through battery power on his flashlight reading in bed. "Even then," Eric thought out loud, "I should give it an extra hour or two. Just to be safe." As much as he wanted to leap from bed the moment he heard his mom close the door to her bedroom, he knew some patience in the matter was best.

Besides, it gave him even more time to study the story of Tocho and just what he and Heather might face when they went out tonight. There were phrases written in the book that he could barely read; considering the events found within the pages, Eric assumed they were from Tocho's native language, perhaps even the words she had used to confront the beast the local kids had come to call Hairy Baby.

"Such a stupid name." Again, speaking to no one, Eric rambled on as he flipped through the book. "I mean, who would think to name a monster Hairy Baby? I know the translations aren't easy, but really? That's the best the locals could come up with?" He kept going over the plan in his head. It was rather simple, as he knew all the best plans were. He would sneak out his window, fairly easy, considering he lived in a single-story house. Another benefit of living in a dense forest was the real concern about fires and the ability to escape the inferno from any location. As such, almost every house in Ashen Forests Estates came with incredibly easy-to-pop-out screens. From the outside you had to all but pry them with a crowbar, but from within, it only took a flick of a small plastic tab and the screen popped right out. No muss. No fuss. He just had to remember to put it back exactly as it was. The house was so new that either parent would be able to tell if something was broken. From there, he'd sneak across the street to Heather's house and gently tap on her bedroom window. He already knew Mrs. Foster's room was on the other side of the haphazardly-built house; she'd never hear them as they went out into the night to find Heather's dog. And maybe, just maybe, the monster that had frightened every kid in the neighborhood for over a hundred years. As adventures went, this one was going to be a doozy.

Eric glanced at his clock, near midnight. "That should do it. No way is mom still awake and dad won't be home for another eight hours." And with that, Eric flung the blankets off his bed. Having already put his regular clothes back on after saying goodnight, it was only a matter of grabbing his flashlight and making his way over to Heather. He flinched a little and instinctively covered his mouth when the window made a louder than expected squeaking sound as he open it fully. He waited for what felt like an eternity, tilting his head to hear if his mom slipped down the hall to his room to check on him. Straining, he only felt the silence of the night. He nodded and went back to the work of getting outside without being heard. The top latch, middle latch, and finally the bottom latch, each one popping open without a care in the world. It was the unexpected boing of the screen flying out of the window frame and onto the ground below that caught his immediate attention. Eric again held himself perfectly still. "Well, good to know how these things work. Efficient little suckers." With that, Eric pulled himself up to the frame, and doing his best to jump with some measure of grace, leapt the few feet to the ground.

"Ugh!" Eric caught himself before even more sounds escaped his mouth as he slammed into the ground outside. While it was true he lived in a single story house, he wasn't thinking about just how high up his window sat until he faced the fall feet first. Even in the daylight, without a single bruise on his body, it would have been a harsh sting on the landing. With the sun on the other side of the planet, he was unable to see the small rock that his already sore feet landed squarely upon, which caused him to promptly drop to his also battered hands and knees. "Keep it together." He nodded to himself; at least he had the good sense to chide himself in muted tones. He improved his grip on his dad's rather thick work flashlight (that he never took to work) and went to switch it on. "Maybe I should keep it off. Just in case. I know this area well enough to move in the dark. Yes, that is a good idea." Eric tried to tell himself that he was speaking out loud because that's what you did on such missions. But he knew the real reason. A small part of him didn't like to think what might be waiting for him out there, beyond what little moonlight pierced the dense forest, fear made even worse by the fact that the strange green glow from within the barn next door was again creeping out from under the cracks. "Just ignore it. It's not what you think it is. Just a barn. Just a barn. There are no tears. Or Tyrs. Or whatever Mr. Gregory said they were. That kind of stuff only happens in the movies, or my books."

Eric slowly made his way over to Heather's house. Again, he kept murmuring to himself. "Sure, just like animal possessing spirits written about by young Native American girls almost a hundred years ago. Sure Eric, that makes total sense." In that short moment Eric started to wonder if, maybe, he was letting his imagination run away with him. He shook it off. That didn't matter. He promised Heather they would look for her dog tonight and that's exactly what he was going to do.

In no time at all Eric made his way to the junk car lot that was Heather Foster's house. Glancing about and acting like every sneaky character he ever saw on television, Eric made his way to the window that opened to Heather's room. He lifted his hand and gently tapped on her window. Nothing. "Come on," he whispered to himself. Again, he tapped a bit louder. And again, there was nary a peep or sign of movement from within. He tried to stand on his toes to see if he could look inside. For once he was glad for his rather short stature as he realized just how creepy that had to look. Even if she was expecting him, it was just weird. Thinking maybe his hand wasn't making a loud enough sound, he lifted the metal-cased flashlight and did his best to tap on the window frame without making too much noise. And, in the weakest yet most audible tone possible, Eric called out. "Heather. Heather, its me. Let's get going."

Eric was so fixated on his attempt at waking his friend that he completely missed the figure slowly approaching him from behind. Again, he tapped on the window and did his best whisper-shout. "Heather! Its meeeee!" He jumped and yelped when a voice from behind answered him.

"What the heck out you doing out here?"

Eric spun around and dropped his flashlight. His eyes wide open, he felt a hand cover his mouth to suppress what was likely another scream, this one loud enough to wake anyone within thirty feet of him. There stood his only friend and she did not look amused. The beam from the dropped flashlight cast a massive shadow of the figure standing before him. She was tall enough without optics adding to her height. It only added to her annoyed appearance. Eric started to move his mouth and realized Heather was still covering it. She looked at him. "Are you going to stop yelling?"

Eric nodded. She let go. And again, she asked what he was doing, using words he was certain she picked up from her mother.

"Remember, we're going out to look for your dog tonight?"

Heather slumped her shoulders forward in genuine shock.

"You were serious about that?"

Now it was Eric's turn to look shocked.

"You weren't? I mean, don't you want to find him?"

Heather replied in earnest. "Of course I do, but, Eric, it's past midnight. Do you really think we can find him in pitch black?"

Eric only mumbled in reply, "I brought my best flashlight. Sucker is strong."

Heather bent over and picked it up. "I can see that." She gave the end a slight twist and the beam grew in intensity. "Whew, you aren't kidding. Wow, this sucker is strong. But that's not the point. I mean, who goes searching for a missing dog in the middle of the night?"

To this Eric had a reply ready, just in case she tried to back out.

"People that are trying to avoid neighborhood bullies with a nasty grudge."

Heather looked at her friend for a few seconds. Eric could tell she was trying to formulate a response. For a brief moment he thought she was going to tell him to go home and go back to bed when suddenly, she said,

"Good point. Let me run in, change, and get a couple things. I'll be back in just a few minutes."

Eric nodded. "Should I come in?"

Heather shook her head. "Naw. My mom is a really heavy sleeper, but this old house creaks and groans like you wouldn't believe. But, if you know where to step, you can keep quiet."

Eric replied with a simple, "Got it."

Heather walked back inside, and it was only then that Eric noticed she was still wearing the same clothes she had on the day before. And when she came out, she was still wearing the same clothes, although with thicker shoes and her own flashlight. Eric couldn't help but tease her a little. "Do you even own a different shirt?"

She popped him on the back of his head. "Shut up, shorty." She turned on her flashlight and together they aimed into the dense woods. "So, where should we look first?"

Eric smiled. "I have some ideas." And with that they walked out into dark woods surrounding Ashen Forest Estates.

Eric and Heather traveled with their thin beams of light for what felt like hours. Together they moved about a forest they called home, yet at this dark hour, it felt more alien than any otherworld location. Sounds that would normally go unnoticed by anyone were now cause to halt in their tracks and look deep for the source. Every once in a while the source of the sound would reveal itself to be a simple bird or even a mouse moving through the brush. In those moments, both kids would look at each other and smile. Yet it was the time when they couldn't find the source that each began to question the intelligence of such a dark adventure.

"Eric, I know you mean well and all. And I really do want to find Hoss, but I think we're going to get in trouble if we keep poking around this place in the dark." As if in reply to Heather's concerns, a much larger creature barked and howled in the night; the pair could not tell the direction it had come from. Heather cleared her throat and grabbed Eric by his arm. "Or something worse."

Eric turned to face his friend, who was merely vocalizing the very concern he was starting to feel.

"You might be right. But how else are we going to find him? I mean, if we go out during the day, Rusty and his sidekick will just go after us again. We got lucky last time; we aren't going to get lucky again."

Heather replied, "Lucky? I don't have a bike the works anymore."

Eric merely nodded and said, "That's what I mean. Just having your bike trashed was us getting lucky. Think about what Rusty could have done. He doesn't strike me as a guy that won't hit a girl. Look, if you want to stop, that is okay with me. We can try and find another way. I mean, I am sure my mom will help us print more fliers. Maybe even drive us around the neighborhood."

Heather looked a little relieved at his suggestion.

"You know, you could have saved me a nice scare tonight if you'd just said that earlier instead of going out on this crazy adventure of yours."

Eric didn't know what to say, save that it might be time to let Heather know the real reason he'd wanted to go out after the sun went down.

"Okay, let's head back. But can we check one more place before we both head inside for the night?"

Heather shrugged. "I guess, but what's the point?"

Eric cleared his throat. "You'll see when we get there."

He could tell his answer was not something Heather liked all that much. He could tell she was starting to grow annoyed at his well-meaning, if misguided ways. After mumbling yet another phrase he was certain she'd picked up from her mom, Heather moved in front of Eric and stood her ground. "This has to do with that stupid book, doesn't it?"

Eric could have lied, but knew there was no point. And besides, for all his crazy talk, he wanted Heather to believe him. So it was time to be 100% honest with her.

"Yes, it does."

Heather started to turn around and make a direct line for her house. Eric shouted at her, "Dang it, listen to me!"

She slowed her pace and turned to face Eric. There was real anger on her face, but Eric's outburst was the closest she had ever heard him get to a real curse. The outburst kept her attention on him. "Fine. You've got five minutes to convince me, or I go home and really think about how much I want to keep hanging out with you."

Eric turned his eyes from Heather. These scenes always seemed so much simpler in his books or movies. The hero gives an epic speech, the music swells, the gang of followers raise their fists to the sky, and they all charge off to glory. Something told Eric this was not how their conversation was going to go. Heather solidified that thought with a simple statement: "Four and a half minutes."

Eric took a few steps closer to her and took the book out of his pocket. "I know it seems crazy, but I am convinced what happened to your dog has happened before. I don't think he's just gone missing. And I also don't think he's the first."

Heather didn't seem all that swayed. "First what? Pet to go missing? Yeah, smart work there, Sherlock. Pets go missing."

Eric flinched a bit at her barb. He was reminded of just how sharp his friend could be if you were on the receiving end of her rather nasty sarcasm.

"They didn't just vanish. They changed. You said yourself when we first met—that dog that chased me. That was never something it had done in the past." Eric tried to push his point even harder. "So, why start then? And why was a dog that's normally all bark turn into some ravenous beast?" This was

150 WELCOME TO GRIZZLYDALE

it; Eric knew there was no going back on his theory. "Because it all happened before. In this book. Written by a girl named Tocho. She'd been through all of this before. And now, so are we!"

Heather raised her voice as high as she felt was safe in the still night air of Ashen Forest Estates. "You're nuts, Eric. Hoss didn't get possessed by some ancient volcano spirit! He got scared; he got out. He's out there, somewhere. Probably scared. And you've got me chasing the neighborhood Bogey Man. Geez. Your mom is right; you need to start growing up. This whole 'let's go on adventures and make believe' is fun, but that's all it is. Fun." Heather started to pace around Eric. "I don't even know what I'm doing out here! You're just a kid. A little kid. Here I am. No real friends. About to enter junior high. Do I go find some girls, some boys? No, I decide to hang out with the neighborhood dork. My mom's right; I am an idiot."

Eric was going to push his case till Heather fired off that final line. He did his best to hide the hurt, the pain that was quickly rising from the pit of his stomach, threatening to spill out from his face. He knew he tended to wear his heart on his sleeve. He was pretty certain the last thing his only friend wanted to see was him crying like the fool she clearly thought he was. He looked down at the book. Against his will, a single tear landed on it and was quickly absorbed into the old leather binding. Eric quietly mumbled to himself, "I guess I deserve that."

Heather turned toward him, any anger she was feeling slowly giving way to regret. Out of anger or not, she was now regretting her choice of words.

"Eric, I... I didn't mean... I don't think you're the..."

Eric cut her off. "The neighborhood dork? Sure you do, because that's what I am. That's what I've always been. That's who I will always be. Making one friend wasn't going to change that."

Heather didn't know what to say. She really did like Eric. "I'm just so worried, Eric. My dog is gone. My mom is working more hours than ever. And when she is home, she's just so tired, and the rare times when she isn't tired, she's mad." Eric pulled the book in closer to his chest, as if the very pages could give him strength. She continued, "And for some stupid reason, you make me forget all that. You remind me what it's like to just have fun". Heather cleared her throat and turned her head towards the ground. "Look, can we just forget what I said? I didn't mean it. I really didn't."

Eric, still holding the book close to his chest, looked back at his friend. He softly nodded; at himself or his friend, even he didn't quite know. Heather took his movement as a nod of agreement. Not wanting more awkwardness, she tried to turn back to the situation at hand. "Look, tomorrow, you and I will go through that book of yours. I mean, we can really dig into it. Shoot, maybe you're right. Maybe there is something to it." Again, Eric slowly nodded as they made their way back to their homes. Heather kept talking as if the constant sound would keep away the pain they both felt which neither friend knew how to process. "You're right, you know. There are all kinds of weird things around the place. Shoot, you really do live next to the single creepiest spot in all of Ashen Forests. Maybe even all of Grizzlydale."

Eric nodded once more, but this time a faint, "I know,"

escaped his lips. They made their way to their houses. Both stood in the middle of the street. Heather slowed her rambling and looked at her friend. "I really am sorry. What I said was mean. I shouldn't have said it. You've been a great friend and I hope we stay that way for a very long time."

With that, Heather wrapped her arms around him and gave him the kind of hug he only thought possible from family members. In that moment, he really did believe her. As she stepped away, he smiled and said,

"This will all work out. I know it will."

Heather smiled back, "I know, too."

She started to make her way back to her house. Eric stood in the street for a few more seconds and then turned, though not back to his house. Without missing a step, Eric began to stride directly toward the barn every kid since the very founding of Ashen Forest Estates knew to avoid when the sun went down.

He barely slowed his pace as he reached for the still-unlocked door and pulled it open. Were it not for the creak that caught Heather's attention, she never would have seen her friend go inside. She turned with speed and raced her way back to Eric.

"What are you doing? Stop! Eric. No. No. No!"

She watched her friend walk into the barn.

Eric gave out a yell that she didn't believe a human could make. There was a flash of green light that illuminated the trees around her.

Heather stood in the dark entrance to the barn.

Eric, her only real friend, was nowhere to be seen.

14
INTO THE TYR

Eric wasn't sure what to expect when he stepped into the barn. If he was being honest, he didn't even understand what compelled him to make the choice. He was even more confused when he walked straight to the glowing green light that had been making his nights so restless. The thing he surely didn't expect, in all his wildest imaginations, was to feel the pull of another arm yanking him to the ground and slamming him into the dirt with as much force as his first bike crash. He hoped the shriek he gave out didn't cause Heather to run in after him. Or worse yet, wake his mother. That would truly be the end of the world. He tried to get up and gather his bearings when he realized his body was pinned down by a rather heavy weight.

"Ugh, I can't breathe!" Eric did his best to move from under the pressure, but whoever or whatever had him was quite skilled in holding down a squirming prey. Immediately his mind went to the utter horror of being lured into the barn by Rusty. "Oh, no. No! We're sorry. We didn't mean—!" His cries were cut off by a hand clasping over his mouth. He could tell by the smell and even taste (which Eric tried his best not to think about) the hand hadn't been washed in some time, or, at the very least, had recently been engaged in all manner of work outside. But it wasn't wholly unpleasant. It smelled a lot like a summer day, with grass and dirt mixed in with sweat. He cursed himself for allowing his mind to wander with poetic notions of a summer day while his body was trapped in what was clearly the most elaborately designed game of revenge ever devised.

Slowly, he opened his eyes. It wasn't as dark as the night sky he and Heather had been under just minutes before. Stranger still was the green hue that covered everything he looked upon. He started to move his mouth again in an attempt to speak, and again, the hand that held him fast clamped down more forcefully. Eric tried to twitch his small frame enough to at least see the face of the bully that was no doubt ready to deliver some swift vengeance on him. While Eric wasn't able to move his whole body from the force holding him down, he was able to move enough to allow his eyes to turn and look at his attacker. It was not what he expected.

"Guh. Gurl," was the best he could mumble as his eyes widened in surprise.

From his limited gaze, he saw just who was holding him down with such skill that even his best squirming couldn't break free. She wasn't dressed like anyone Eric had ever seen before. Her clothes were simple cloth and leathers, like something out of his fantasy book. But unlike his books, her clothing didn't look like a costume piece. These were well lived-in and cared-for items. He looked down to the hand holding his mouth shut. It was a small hand, but with real strength behind it. Furthermore, this girl had the hands of someone that spent a lot of time outside. Although he couldn't tell her exact age, he doubted she was more than a couple of years older than Heather. These were hands that did not spend their days holding a game controller, or really any mundane indoor item. Looking up at her, Eric noticed she was barely paying attention to him. Her gaze fixed sternly upon whatever was beyond the large rock they were both crouched behind, she by design, and he by her will alone. There was a determination in her eyes that he had only seen once or twice in the past. Neither was a pleasant memory. He'd read a lot of books about mother bears or wolves driving off entire groups of hunters or predators when their offspring were threatened, that there was nothing more dangerous than a parental figure going to the ends of the Earth to protect their young. The focused attention of the older girl now holding him down carried that very look. Eric found it rather comforting, if a little scary. Slowly, her eyes shifted from whatever had her attention to Eric. She did not looked amused.

"...Who... Are... Boy," was all Eric understood. What he understood more was the nasty gaze she was now giving him. Slowly, she let some of the pressure off his body, and Eric gave a rather loud inhale of air through his nose. Immediately, the girl placed her index finger to her mouth in the universal sign for "keep quiet." Eric slowly nodded and his brain went into overdrive. He couldn't understand her, which meant she probably couldn't understand him. But she was clearly smart enough to know how to sign with him, which meant that they had some form of common ground, for all the good that might do. Taking a shot, Eric moved his hand slowly to his mouth and, gesturing with his finger, visually asked if she could please remove her hand. She eyed him suspiciously, then slowly moved her hand off of him. Eric wasn't sure what to do next. She was still leaning uncomfortably close to him. It was then that he noticed a rather sharp-looking axe not a few inches from her hand on the ground. His eyes grew, both in understanding and a little fear. He was starting to figure out what was happening, although even his fantasy-based mind was having a hard time allowing the idea. Deciding to instead focus on the moment, Eric slowly slid himself to a sitting position. The girl kept her attention on him while sometimes glancing over the rock. Eric gently cleared his throat and whispered,

"Thank you."

The girl looked at him and nodded. Eric wasn't sure if she understood what he meant or was simply giving whatever reply she thought most appropriate. His curiosity was ended when she replied.

"Who are you?"

Her voice, like much of her countenance, suggested someone that was far older than her size. Eric has heard his grandma talk about people with old souls. He never really knew what that meant until this very moment. This girl, whomever she was, had already seen far more than most that live complete lifetimes. Her accent was unfamiliar to him. Not hard to understand in the least, but unlike any he'd ever heard before.

"Eric. "

She sat back a bit from her almost predatory position. She

kept looking him over, as if something new would pop out if she stared long enough. Finally, she responded to his simple reply.

"You do not look like them".

Eric wasn't sure how to respond. "'Them' who?"

The girl tilted her head, as if trying to understand just what Eric was asking. Finally, she replied,

"You do not look like my people, nor do you share the color of the settlers. Or their dress."

Eric's eyes grew with immediate understanding. Everything he'd read. The crazy words from Mr. Gregory the librarian. They were all true. Grizzlydale wasn't like any other town. Time. Space. It was all in flux in the town of Grizzlydale and somehow now Eric was a part of that insanity. He swallowed back his excitement. Whatever he said next would have to be important. He couldn't afford for this girl to think he was some nutcase that fell from nowhere. Although thinking that to himself, he wasn't sure there was any way to avoid it. He decided to let it all fall out.

"My name is Eric. I've been trying to help my friend find her dog. All these pets are going missing and no one knows why. Then I find out that I live next to a monster in the green glow. So we go out looking, but not before getting into a fight with Rusty the bully. Oh, and that was after I crashed my bike running from a dog that was totally possessed. Oh, and I know all about that because I have this book that mentions the same monster from a long time ago. Well, maybe not long to you, if I am right. And then I went to the library—shoot, you probably don't know what a library is. I mean, not that you're dumb, you don't look dumb, but do they have libraries yet? I mean, in America? Anyway, Mr. Gregory gets all spooky-looking and tells me about the Tyrs in this town and how all kinds of things come out of them. So I look into the volcano, when I think the first Tyr showed up. And now I think it's right next to my room. So, Heather and I go out, Heather is my friend; you'd like her. We go out and keep looking for her dog, who is still missing. Oh, I am pretty sure her dog—his name is Hoss. Anyway, I am pretty sure Hoss is under the strange influence as well. We still haven't found him. Then we got into a fight because she thinks I'm a little crazy so I walked into the barn with the green glow to prove to her I'm not and then you tackled me."

To her credit, the girl didn't immediately brain Eric with her axe and walk away. Although, if Eric was being honest with himself, she probably didn't understand a tenth of what he just said. Because even he didn't understand. It was as if all the pieces in the strangest puzzle ever decided to fall on the table at once. He couldn't see the image yet, but everything was there. She sat there in awkward silence and didn't answer him. Eric couldn't take the silence anymore. "Um, where am I?"

That, the girl could and did answer.

"You are in my land. And you are a very stupid boy,"

Eric couldn't help but roll his eyes at that reply. "Well, tell me something I don't know."

She looked confused. "How would I do that?"

Eric shook his head. "Never mind."

The girl placed her hand on Eric's chest and made him sit absolutely still. He knew better than to ask her what she was doing as he saw her grab her axe with her other hand and tilt her eyes and ears towards the strangely glowing forest. It was only then that the reality of Eric's situation started to set in. "I am in so much trouble."

The girl nodded without looking.

"That, strange boy, is something upon which we can both agree. We are both in much trouble." She lowered her look from the forest and returned to Eric. "I do not know who you are. But you will get us both caught by the beast. You need to leave."

Eric shook his head. "No, I can't. Please. I need to find a way back."

The girl started to stand up, she was clearly going to leave Eric where he sat.

"Leave, small boy. Go your own way. You will only get us both killed." Her stature changed, as if what she just said caused pain inside her small but strong frame. "Just as I have before."

Eric wasn't sure what she meant by that, but he knew he wasn't going to get out of this Tyr without her help. He wasn't sure why he knew that, but everything within him told him this was true.

"Please, I think we need each other."

The girl spun angrily and pointed at Eric with her axe.

"No! No one helps me anymore. No one gets hurt. It is my burden now. I provoked the spirits; I must pay the price." With that, she started to walk away from Eric and into the glowing forest. Eric stood there, unsure what to do next. He was quickly going to be alone in a place he did not know, and very likely, a time he did not know. He looked around for something, anything that might help him prove they should work together. It was then that he noticed the rock they were both hiding behind was the very same rock his parents had moved to place their home. He looked around more. There, to his left, green light shined from a fissure in the ground. He started to walk towards it. Although she was walking away, the girl must have known what he was doing.

"If you touch it, it will burn you. Burn so deep your skin will never heal."

Eric stopped. He looked around. If that was the same massive rock, then this fissure was where his neighbors' barn sat. He was still in Ashen Forest Estates, but it was not his Ashen Forests. Eric reached into his pocket and pulled out his book.

"Hemei Ninambebea." Eric didn't say anything else.

The girl stopped dead in her tracks and turned to face the strange small boy that had come out from the darkness. For the first time, Eric saw real shock on her face. "You're hunting Hemei Ninambebea." She walked with purpose to Eric, the axe firm in her hand. Eric did his best to not cower as she cut the distance between the two of them.

"How do you know that name"? It was more of a demand than a question. Eric wasn't cocky or proud; he merely lifted the book from his side and raised his eyes to face hers.

"The same way I know your name is Tocho and that you don't survive this night."

15
MAKING FRIENDS

Tocho looked deep into Eric's eyes, as if her gaze could find the truth in his words.

"Just what do you mean, I am not going to survive this night?"

Eric cleared his throat. His gamble had worked; now he just needed to sell the rest of his crazy idea. Taking a very small step back from Tocho's intimidating stance, Eric slowly explained his reasons.

"This book. My teacher gave it to me on the last day of school. I think it's about you and what you're doing out here."

Tocho lifted an eyebrow in curiosity.

"And just how are you sure this book is about me?"

Eric nodded as he continued to explain to Tocho. "The book mentions a young Indi, um, a young woman. It mentions a spirit that stalked the land after the volcano erupted. About how this spirit would infect all the creatures of the woods. Make them turn on the men and women that call this forest home."

Tocho relaxed a little. As strange as Eric was sounding, he must have been getting through to her. He kept talking. "I don't know when it happens, but eventually you go out to face the spirit. You have help from some men from your village and a white farmer from what becomes my home, Grizzlydale."

Tocho slowly lowered herself to her knees, as if the words coming from Eric's mouth carried a weight that was too much for her to bear.

"I know it sounds crazy, but the book mentions you and your friends going toward the volcano. To finally confront the spirit. Then, nothing. It just ends. At least, any mention of you. There are a few more pages about rips in the ground and evil finding root in the land itself. But of you, there isn't anything else." Eric, almost by instinct, lowered himself to sit next to the young woman. "And since more animals are disappearing or just attacking people at random in my time ..." Eric choose his next words quite carefully. "Something told me your confrontation against the spirit you call Hemei Ninambebea didn't go so well."

Tocho didn't answer for a few minutes. Eric did his best to not squirm. Better yet, he did his best to not resort to his usual action of filling awkward silence with endless prattle that would only make the situation worse. Instead, they both sat in the eerie silence as green mist floated about the air. As strange as the surroundings were, Eric found the place strangely calming. He stifled a laugh when he realized that the amount of danger he was in now was hundreds of times worse than any neighborhood bully. And yet here he was, without a shred of fear. Perhaps it was the fantasy nature of the event that calmed his nerves, as if years of reading and playing games prepared him for this day. He took some solace in that thought. Now if only the books and games could provide an answer to this event. Better still, a way home. Finally, Tocho broke into his silent thoughts.

"Two days ago, I went up the mountain with some men. As you said, a brave man from my village and an outsider from down the mountain." Tocho looked out into the glowing woods. "I am the only one that returned. The Hemei Ninambebea took them all. It's growing in strength. It's now able to take the body of a person and make him its slave. It took the white man first. He did his best to fight the dark spirit, but there is no way to repel the Hemei Ninambebea. Once it enters you, you are forever lost to its evil ways. Forever cursed to cause pain and suffering on those you once called friend and family."

Eric sat up straight. This did not sound good, and no amount of reading could prepare him for the idea of his friends or family turning into monsters. Tocho kept talking. "We let it chase us back down the mountain. For what seemed like days, it played with us. Sometimes, when the sun tried to pierce the ash that covered the sun, we could hear the white man scream in pain. As if he were fighting the spirit from within. But all too soon, the sun would again go behind a cloud, or the cover of night, and the man was gone. There was only Hemei Ninambebea."

Eric was starting to understand where this was going. He looked at Tocho and said,

"That's why your story ends in the book. You did it.

Somehow, you killed the spirit."

Tocho shook her head.

"You cannot kill that which was never truly alive. The Hemei Ninambebea exists between all worlds. It does not live, nor does it die."

She stopped her statement quickly as a hollow echo deep in the woods caught their attention. For an agonizing amount of time, both Tocho and Eric strained to listen further. Nothing came from the deep woods. She continued to tell her story.

"We brought it to a pit trap. One of the village hunters would use them to bring down very large prey. Taking what knowledge Honi and I gained from our elders, we were able to lure the possessed white man into the pit." Her voice grew weak and Eric noticed she was starting to shiver. She was doing her best to keep her composure. Eric was tempted to place his hand on her shoulder, as he would do with his mom or even Heather were either of them in such a state. He decided to keep his hands at his sides around Tocho. Something about what she was going through told him that it was something she had to work through on her own. She gathered herself and kept talking.

"Honi, my friend, jumped into the pit and kept the man that was Hemei Ninambebea busy as I prepared the spells. There was so little left of the white man. His form was twisted. A mockery of all that is good with creation. Even now, I cannot explain to you the horrors that I saw in that pit. And my friend. He fought bravely. He didn't have a single hunt to his name. But that night—that night he did all our ancestors proud. There was a flash and then—then." Tocho cleared her throat again. "It was done. The spell worked. Hemei

Ninambebea was frozen in place. I took the sheets with the holy words and threw them into the pit. The Hemei Ninambebea screamed but did not move." Tocho slowly got to her feet. "And then I spent the rest of the day filling the pit with stone and dirt." She looked around her and then looked back to Eric. "That was the day I trapped Hemei Ninambebea in a pit. Never to return."

Eric looked at Tocho, the stillness in the air maddening to him. Before long, Eric broke the silence.

"We call it Hairy Baby."

Tocho looked at Eric in confusion.

"What?"

Eric nodded and said the name again. "Something tells me the neighborhood Bogey Man that's been scaring kids for decades is the very same monster that consumed your friends and infected this land."

Tocho shook her head.

"That is not the same name. Why would we fear a baby covered in hair?"

Eric smiled and replied, "No, I think that's what the locals started calling it. Once your people..." Eric's words trailed off. For the first time since being pulled into whatever world this was, he felt scared. Scared and sad. He knew the history of his town. While there were still many of Tocho's tribe in Grizzlydale, sitting there now, seeing her face, he knew that her people would never be the same. Be it from the settlers that took more and more land, or the beast he was now trying to put down, Tocho's people were forever changed. He hoped she wouldn't ask why he paused as he continued to talk with her. "The men and women of Grizzlydale never learned to speak your language. But many of your myths and legends still live. I think what you call Hemei Ninambebea, we started to call Hairy Baby. A stupid name about a very real monster I think most people forgot about."

Tocho still didn't seem to understand.

"Eric. If what you say is true, if you are from a time beyond my own, if you say the Hemei Ninambebea is now but a child's tale, then that means I was victorious. That the spirit was indeed put down."

Eric slowly shook his head.

"I don't think you defeated it. I think you just trapped it—weakened it so much that it stayed trapped. But not completely. I think a small part of its energy was able to escape. Just enough to frighten kids in the middle of the night. Enough to keep its legend alive and well."

Tocho nodded.

"Perhaps what you say is true. That the Hemei Ninambebea, or Hairy Baby, was trapped. What happened? Why does it now grow in power? Why are you here?"

This was the part of the explanation that Eric was not looking forward to.

"Because I think when my family moved in, we weakened your trap. I started to see a green glow, just like the fissures that cut into this dark forest." Tocho's expression slowly turned to one of shock. "I think the spirit is slowly escaping, in my time."

Tocho grasped Eric by his collar and pulled him in tight.

"Haven't you been listening? The Hemei Ninambebea doesn't live like you and I. It can come and grow through the cracks in the ground as simply as you and I walk through rivers. If you freed it in your time, then all that I did—all of it for nothing! It simply gains power. Grows all around us. Around me. My people!" She pushed Eric to the ground. He didn't know what to say. She was right. While it wasn't his fault directly, he still knew that he was part of the reason the spirit again walked both their worlds. Why she would have no rest after her horrible ordeal. He looked up at Tocho from the ground.

"That's why I walked into a Tyr."

Tocho shook her head. "What are you talking about? What is a Tyr?"

Eric started to stand. "That's what they call the cracks in the ground in my time. Or, at least that's what the creepy librarian called them." Eric didn't hear Tocho's reply, his mind racing as pieces started to fall into place. His strange encounter with Mr. Gregory started to make more sense. He'd known exactly what Eric was looking for, and yet made no attempt to help him. He needed Eric to learn about the Tyrs and legend of the Hemei Ninambebea all on his own. The only question that truly eluded him was the why. Why would Mr. Gregory want him to learn of the monstrous stories behind Grizzlydale all on his own? Then, he remembered the librarian's words just before his mom arrived. Without even noticing, Eric spoke them aloud. "You might be the one."

Tocho caught his attention.

"One what?!"

He could tell she was growing more and more angry. He rubbed his eyes in desperation and told her more.

"Next to my home. There is one of these cracks. Or Tyrs as they're known. My friend and I went out to find her lost dog.

I think the Hairy Baby is influencing all the animals in the neighborhood. We got into a fight. But, instead of going home, something told me to walk into the Tyr. Which brought me here. To you." Tocho seemed to calm a little. "And I don't think that was an accident."

Tocho bent down and grabbed the axe she had dropped.

"And just what am I supposed to do? Follow you?"

Eric shook his head.

"No. From what I read in this book, if you step into a Tyr, you'll be lost in time, just like the stranger at the beginning."

Tocho stiffened up at the mention of the strangers.

"Let me guess, you read about this strange boy as well."

Eric nodded.

"Yes. I don't know quite how he fits in with what I need to do, but I have an idea where I can find out."

In the distance, there was another howl, this one closer. Tocho placed herself between Eric and the sound. Eric, though nervous, didn't stop talking. "Tocho, I need to know how you trapped the spirit the first time. Please."

Tocho turned to face Eric. Again, her eyes looked deep into him. It was hard to tell, but he could swear he saw the faintest of smiles cross her face. She leaned in and whispered to him what he would need to again trap the Hemei Ninambebea. Eric took out the book. It pained him to do so, but he wrote down her words as best as he could in the back of the book. Then, he closed it and put it back into his pocket.

Together, they moved slowly back toward the glowing green Tyr where Eric first appeared and where Tocho almost tossed an axe into his forehead.

Eric nodded with determination and started to make his

way into the Tyr. He turned to Tocho. "Okay, when this is done, I will come back. I will visit you. Maybe we can find a way to get you out of here."

Tocho smiled at him. "You are a strange little boy."

Eric smiled back. "You aren't the first person to tell me that."

With that, he stepped into the Tyr and vanished from the bizarre area. Eric was so thrilled at having a way to fight the evil in both times, he was completely oblivious to the fact that Tocho spoke his last name. A last name that he never told her.

From the woods, another howl. Tocho steadied herself and then spoke.

"That's enough. He's gone."

From the glowing edges of the woods, a much older Eric Del Bosque stepped out and gave Tocho a solemn smile. Tocho did not return the smile.

"We should have told him," she said.

Older Eric shook his head.

"No. Now is not the time. The truth will come to him soon enough, as it did me."

Tocho did not agree. "It doesn't make it right."

Again, Eric shook his head.

"What is right and what must be done are two very different things in the town of Grizzlydale."

16
BACK AT THE BARN

Heather stood in the open door to the barn. The barn that every kid in Ashen Forest Estates knew to avoid. Even when the sun provided a false sense of security, everyone knew this was a building to be avoided. And yet here she was. At the very peak of the night sky, standing in its open door. Worse still, her only real friend in a very long time had just stepped inside and with a muffled scream, was gone.

She whispered, "Eric? Eric I'm sorry, okay. Please, Eric, please stop goofing around." She leaned inside just a bit, only a few inches, with her legs quite firm in their placement. But those few inches her torso and head leaned in felt like miles. In fact, with any other neighborhood kid around, her actions at the door would have earned her the placement as the bravest (or most foolish) kid in Ashen Forest. Still, Heather saw nothing. Years of living in a home that was less than supportive caused her to resort to learned emotions and actions. Her immediate worry for her friend quickly turned to anger as a part of her felt Eric was just one more person trying to teach her a lesson at the expensive of her feelings.

"Fine, you made your point. And you know what? I don't care. I was stupid to think you'd be any different than the rest of them." She backed away from the door. Although part of her wanted to dramatically spin and walk back to her house in anger, there was a stronger part that wholly believed every story about that barn and the creature that lived within. Stories that demanded she not even dare turn her back to whatever could come leaping from the darkness. As she backed up, Heather grasped the open door and slammed it shut. The sound of the wooden door impacting the frame echoed throughout Ashen Forests Estates. In the distance, one or two dogs began barking, which led to a cascade of animals that threatened to wake up everyone. Heather stood completely still and held her breath. A few moments passed and she allowed herself a silent exhale. For good or bad, barking in the middle of the night was an all too common occurrence where she lived, and unless those barks were accompanied by shouts or screeching tires, most people just rolled over and went back to sleep.

Still she stared at the barn. Almost five minutes had passed since Eric silently walked through the dark doorway. Heather made a small step back to the barn. In the short time that she and Eric had known each other, she had learned that he was many things. He was weird. He was prone to flights of fancy. He even had a tendency to stretch the truth if it made for a good story. But of all the things he was, Heather knew deep down that her friend was not a mean person. Sure, he might play a quick joke on her. But something like this? Something that went so very deep into her fears?

"No, that is not Eric. That is not my friend." She took a few more steps into the barn. Heather came to the one and only conclusion. Something had happened to Eric when he walked into that barn. Maybe there was no such thing as Hairy Baby. But that didn't mean there weren't plenty of situations where he was lying on the floor in a nasty barn, unable to speak or cry out for help. With that, Heather double checked her flashlight, tugged on her shirt, and made her way through the barn door. Her hand shook ever so slightly as she reached for the handle.

"Okay, Heather, you can do this. Don't think about the stories. It's just a barn. It isn't any different at night than in the day. It's just a stupid barn." And with that, Heather pulled on the handle. The creak of the hinges sounded loud in her hyper-aware ears, but to anyone else, it was just trees swaying in a gentle breeze.

Taking a deep breath, Heather steadied herself and stepped into the barn. Her flashlight did little to pierce a darkness that felt thick. "Okay, Eric, wherever you are, I'm going to find you." Stopping a moment after taking her first steps in, Heather looked around. She was honestly a little shocked to find that the only thing special about this barn was that it was anything but. Only a few tools hung on the walls or were strewn about on the floor. There was no large machinery kept inside to protect it from the elements. Nothing but oddly placed walls here and there, as if there was a time when this barn was going to hold horses or other form of livestock and the builder simply stopped working. The floor was remarkably clean. She shrugged. "I mean, I wouldn't eat off it, but I'm pretty sure this barn is cleaner than most mudrooms in this town." She took a few more steps in. When she was relatively certain her voice wouldn't carry far beyond the open door, Heather starting calling out to her friend. "Eric. Eric, it's me." She walked further into the barn. Passing the first set of half-walls, she saw a faint glimmer of light in what she assumed was the far corner of the barn. It was hard to tell from her distance. A voice inside her was already telling her to get out, to wake up Eric's parents, no matter what form of punishment she would face. Heather's determination grew. No. She wasn't going to include parents until she was absolutely certain they were needed. Perhaps it was a bit selfish to think that way, but Heather smiled at the thought that her friend would think the exact same thing. For good or bad, she and Eric had a lot in common. They would see this through, together. Slowly, she made her way to the faint light. "Eric, is that you? If you can't talk, can you move the light a little? So I know it's you."

She waited a minute or two. No sounds or movement from the area of the light. The voice telling her to run grew louder still. "No," she said out loud. "It's just a stupid barn." With determination she hadn't felt in a long time, Heather strode with purpose toward the light. Steeling herself for whatever she found, Heather rounded the second set of half-walls to face the light source. As she rounded the corner, she started to talk.

"You really had me, Eric. I was angry at first, but I figured you got hurt, so you'll be glad to know I also faced the terrors of Hairy Baby's lair and—" Her voice cut off instantly as she rounded the corner. Her body and voice froze as she faced the one thing she was absolutely not prepared for. There, sitting in the furthermost corner of the barn, sat Eric's flashlight. Or at least, half of his flashlight. The lens was barely peeking out from under the cracked stone floor that covered most of this corner of the barn. Fear locked her body in place.

"Eric?" She couldn't move as she stared at the light. It wasn't buried in some dirt and sticking out. It looked as if someone had gently balanced her friend's flashlight in the ground, and then poured cement over it, locking it forever inside the stone floor, but just enough so that it wouldn't cover the whole thing. Somehow, against all her instincts, Heather took a few more steps to what was left of Eric's flashlight. The gentle glow illuminated her face. She reached out and touched the visible portion of the flashlight. It was ice cold. "Eric? Please. Where are you?" Outside, she heard movement. Heather was so far inside the barn she couldn't tell from exactly where the movement was coming from. The horror of the situation finally set in. Without thinking, Heather dropped her own light and bolted from the horrible scene of a missing friend and a trapped light. Losing her footing, Heather slammed into one of the half-walls in the barn. She let out a shriek and fell from the impact. She felt something warm start to drip from her nose. Heather didn't need a light to know she'd hurt herself pretty bad. Outside, she heard something sniff. She did her best to stifle a cry. It wasn't enough. Whatever was outside had slowly made its way to the opening of the barn. It sounded large. The sniffing sounded like a shout in her ears. Mixed in with her utter terror, Heather felt a twinge of anger. It had been a long time since she'd felt completely powerless in an event beyond her control. She forced herself to stand.

"No. Whatever the heck you are, you're not getting this girl without a fight." But even as she said it, Heather doubted her own words. She was tired. She was hurt. She was more scared than she could ever recall. And, in the back of her mind, she was frightened that whatever took her only friend from this world was now making its way to her. The sniffing grew louder still. Seconds passed. Then, the faint glow from her dropped light revealed a image she had known for most of her life. There, standing before her, was Hoss. Her oldest and best friend in the whole world. She let out a nervous laugh and slowly reached out her hand. "Hey, boy. Where have you been?"

The dog pulled back, its teeth baring in the most vicious growl Heather had ever seen. Fear washed over her as she looked into her pet's eyes to see an eerie green glow, the same green glow kids had talked about for decades, the same green glow Eric was convinced was tied to the legendary Hairy Baby. Heather could only whimper to her longtime companion as it methodically approached her, its mouth a pit of sharp teeth and horrible liquid.

"Please," was all Heather could muster as it came within arm's reach of her. To her credit, Heather never once closed her eyes.

Heather waited for the stabbing pain brought on by her beloved pet.

It never came. Instead, bright light shone through the cracks of the barn from outside and she heard a familiar sound.

"Heather! Heather, where are you?"

She didn't care that it was probably loud enough to wake

whoever was sleeping in the nearby homes. She knew the sound of her friend Eric's voice, and it was the most welcome sound she could have ever imagined.

"Eric? In the barn. Help, it's in here with me!"

Eric rushed to the open door. Heather's possessed pet turned its head to face Eric as he made his way into the entry. A shot of courage ran though Heather and she charged her pet. The dog let out a sound she'd never heard it make before. More guttural roar than a growl or bark, it again turned its attention to her. From just a few feet away Heather heard her friend Eric let out some words that he probably picked up from her. Without even thinking, a part of her smiled and felt some pride that her less than savory language was catching and if they lived through this, she would have to tease him about it.

Eric lifted the book into the air and started speaking in a language she'd never heard before. In fact, to Heather, it simply sounded like nerdy gibberish. Her eyes widened as she saw her dog turn its full attention to Eric and charge at him with supernatural speed. There was simply no time to stop it. Her beloved pet was going to make hamburger out of her friend.

"Nooooooo!" she cried out, her hands reaching out to Eric. In a panic, Eric dropped the book. What had started as a simple and, quite honestly, dumb quest to find her missing pet had turned into a disaster that no one could have predicted.

Eric did his best to shield his face from the oncoming horror of teeth and claws. He felt the impact that sent him flying back outside, but the expected bite never came. Instead, he heard Heather call out his name from within the barn. Eric broke the silence and yelled from within the barn,

"Um, I am pretty sure I am dead now."

From within the barn, Eric heard Heather reply.

"I think we both are, or should be."

He moved his hands from his face. The dog was nowhere to be seen. Eric sat up, but made no attempt to stand. From in the barn, he saw Heather slowly make her way outside.

"That was Hoss. That was my dog, my buddy."

Eric shook his head.

"It was, but not anymore. That was Hemei Ninambebea."

Heather plopped herself onto the ground in front of Eric. The tears started to come, and she clearly didn't care if Eric saw them. Eric looked at his friend. This time he didn't stay silent. Eric scooted himself closer to his friend and put his arm around her. "You haven't given up on me, so I'm not ready to give up on you. On Hoss". If the situation wasn't so serious, they would both be laughing at Eric's tiny arm trying to get around Heather's rather broad shoulders. Instead, she simply leaned her head on his shoulder and through the tears asked, "What now?"

Eric took a deep breath.

"Now? Now we both go home and try and sleep. Tomorrow? Tomorrow we have a lot to talk about and even more to do."

He helped Heather up and together made their way back to her house. Her tears had passed and in the faint moonlight he saw her face.

"Wow, what happened?"

Heather looked at him for a moment and then realized she must look like a horror movie victim with her face a mix of tears, a bloody nose, and a rather unsettling amount of snot that flows out when you face your beloved pet that was now possessed by some evil spirit. She did her best to smile back at him.

"It's not as bad as it looks. I just need to get cleaned up and in bed before my mom wakes up." She poked Eric in the shoulder. "You should too." Eric nodded. They stood before Heather's front door. She reached out and pulled Eric into a hug. It was warm and felt safe. For both of them.

"I'm sorry, Eric. I really am."

Eric hugged her back.

"Me too. I promise, Heather, together we will figure out what's going on and stop it."

Heather pulled away and smiled.

"I believe you. Now go home and sleep. Like you said, busy day tomorrow."

And like that, the strong-as-nails thirteen-year-old girl that saved him the first day he went riding in Ashen Forests Estates was back.

"You got it."

Both made it home without getting caught, but while they were both able to clean up and crawl into bed, sleep came for neither of them.

17
THE DAY AFTER

What was left of the night seemed to take forever to pass as Eric lay still in his bed. His mind couldn't shut out the images of what he experienced. Even his incredibly active imagination was having a hard time believing in his night. He could still hear Tocho's voice in his ear. But it was no longer the strong and vibrant voice of the young woman. Instead, merely an echo of Tocho, as if the very act of passing through a Tyr and into his own time and space had separated his memories. Eric felt a temptation to look back out his window, at the barn that had changed both he and his friend's life forever. The events were too fresh in his mind. He couldn't bring himself to look back out, to look out and remind himself that he must again face whatever horrors used the barn as a gateway into his world.

"All myths have a spark of truth," was all Eric could mumble to himself. He'd read something similar to those words many times in the past. Even his last teacher, Mrs. Fontana, had said such things to her class. Eric wondered just what his teacher would think of this situation. Then his mind began to wander back over the events that led to this very moment. He sat up in bed, the darkness of his room fully engulfing him.

"Could she have known? Did Ms. Fontana want me to learn about the real secrets of Grizzlydale?" Eric sat completely still. It was not a very good feeling to have. For the whole year before, Ms. Fontana had been a strict but fair teacher. Not only that, but she was one of the rare adults in his life that never once told him to take his nose out of a book. In fact, there were times when she'd let him stay inside while the other kids went outside to the playground. The thought that someone that he looked up to was actively working toward his demise bothered him.

Eric shook his head and again spoke out loud. "Well, now you're just being paranoid." Knowing sleep was not something he would enjoy this night, he still lowered his head onto the small, but soft pillow, providing a welcome relief from the unsettling night.

"Eric, come out here. Now. We need to talk." It was never a good thing when his mom used such a tone first thing in the morning. Truthfully, there was never a good time for that tone, but hearing it in the morning always gave Eric extra pause. Whatever conversation they were about to have could taint the entire day. Indeed, there were more than a few times when such talks altered the very fabric of the week. Still, there was no sense in delaying, or even faking that he was still asleep. If there was one thing his whole family knew to be true, it was that Eric did not sleep like your average kid. Six hours was a marathon resting session and even then, the slightest peep in the house would rouse him. With all that in mind, Eric replied.

"I'll be right there."

Sliding out of his bed, he glanced at himself in the mirror. He was taken back by what he saw. Even in the bright morning sun, he could see a faint glow around his body. Without thinking he tried to brush it away, as if whatever was coating him would flick off with a couple of hand slaps. There was no change. In a panic, Eric rushed over to his dresser and fished out a whole new set of pajamas. "Maybe I still had gunk on me, or some weird Tyr juice. Or—or—eww. Tyr juice is about the worst thing I've ever said." He shivered a bit as he slipped on new clothes.

From outside his room, his mom called to him again.

"I did mean now. As in this morning, Eric."

Eric looked at himself in the mirror again. The glow was still there. Under his breath he mumbled a few choice words he'd picked up from his friend Heather, words he not dare speak around his mom or dad. Again, his mom called out.

"Eric Armando Del Bosque. Now!"

That was it; his full name had been uttered. There was no hiding from whatever waited for him. Maybe telling his mom the truth would help. "Yeah, right," Eric mumbled to himself before saying louder, "Sorry! I'm coming." And with that, Eric left his room and made his way into the kitchen where he hoped his mom was on her second cup of coffee and therefore in a better mood.

Eric rounded the corner and saw that his mom had her back to him. She turned, still stirring what appeared to be her first cup. This was not a good start. She looked at him silently for a few seconds. Eric prepared himself for the inevitable freak out when she saw that her one and only child was glowing like someone had dumped all the contents of Halloween glow sticks over him. Instead, she smiled.

"What took you so long?"

Eric did an honest-to-goodness double take at her question.

"What do you mean, what took me so long?"

Earlina took a sip of her coffee and grinned. "Mijo, you never sleep past eight a.m. and here it is eight-thirty. I was wondering if you were okay." Eric was still slow to answer and that raised her curiosity. "Are you feeling okay? Did you sleep well?"

To this, Eric could answer his mom quite honestly.

"Not really, mom. I kept waking up all night."

His mom took another sip and sat at the kitchen table.

"That's what I wanted to ask you about."

Eric took a deep breath and prepared himself. For some reason, his mom couldn't see the glow covering him, but that didn't mean she was oblivious to what happened last night. The options in his head started to race so quickly he was absolutely certain the only answer he was going to provide would not only be wrong, but also not make a lick of sense. No matter; it was too late now. His mom continued.

"Did you see anything outside your window last night? The neighbors were telling me there were all kinds of strange animals sounds, and someone broke into the barn next door."

Eric did his best to hide his surprise as he steadied himself again the chair and the table. Turning his face from his mom just enough to hide his expression but not seem obvious, he gathered himself and sat at the table with his mom.

"I did hear some strange noises."

Earlina nodded and told him to tell her more.

"To be honest, mom, it was a little scary. So I just turned on my radio and pulled my blankets over my head."

His mom laughed a little. On any other occasion Eric's feelings would be just a little hurt. Although, as a rule, his mom was quite protective and supportive of Eric, she did find some humor in watching others get scared. Her son was not immune to her chuckles. This time, though, Eric was more than happy to let her have a giggle or two if it meant he and Heather were not suspects in the ruckus that apparently had woken up a rather large portion of the neighborhood.

"You know you can always get me, or your dad. Well, mainly me; don't try and wake up your father. You know how he can be."

To that, Eric gave an honest smile. Once his dad's head hit the pillow, nothing short of a full scale invasion would wake him from his slumber. Eric looked down at the table and traced his fingers on the fake wood patterns, taken back at how easily his mind turned woodgrain designs into horrible little faces that snarled back at him. He was always tempted to ask others if they had similar experiences, but like so many other oddities in his life, he was worried to learn it was just him. His mom snapped him out of his lost moment. "You know that, right? I know you're getting older. Even starting a new school in a couple of months. But, you're never too old to come to us when you're scared."

Eric looked back up at his mom. He knew she meant every word. He just wished he could tell her everything. Ask her for help. But deep down he knew, with every fiber of his being, he knew this was something that only he and Heather could take care of.

"I know, mom. This is a little embarrassing, but I was too nervous to leave my bed. The sounds were really creepy."

His mom patted him on the head as she finished her first cup of coffee and made her way to pour a second.

"Well, that's what the neighbor said. He said there might be a couple of animals loose in the area. So I need you to be extra careful out there. And no more staying out once the sun starts to set." Eric let out a sigh that suggested he was not happy about her request. "Don't worry; it won't affect our deal about the chest of books." She sat back down. "Speaking of which, what do you have planned today?"

Eric leaned back in his chair.

"Actually, Heather and I were wondering if you could take us to the library."

Earlina shook her head a bit. "Really, so you can spend hours there just to not check out any books?"

Having collected himself after he realized his mom couldn't see his strange glow, the half-truths came to Eric a little too easily.

"No. We want to get some books on fixing bikes. Heather's mom can't afford a new one, so we want to see if we can fix hers."

His mom took another sip.

"You know, there is this thing called the Internet where you can look all that stuff up and it doesn't cost me the gas money to go into town." Eric started to reply when his mom cut him off. "I'm just teasing. I've got a few errands to run anyway. So yes, I can take you and your friend to the library. Just don't make me wait this time."

Eric smiled.

"Thanks, mom!"

She nodded as she enjoyed the steam rising from her coffee cup. "Oh, has Heather found her dog yet?"

Memories of the night before washed over Eric, and he was unable to hide the sadness that read as plain as day on his face. He didn't bother trying to hide it from his mom.

"No. Not yet. Heather isn't sure how much longer she wants to keep looking. There are a lot of bigger animals out there. And she's... Well, she's trying to stay hopeful."

Earlina didn't say anything. They both knew what Eric meant. She took another sip and did her best to change the subject.

"We'll leave after lunch. Okay"?

Eric nodded and grabbed a bowl of cereal. It was a rather muted breakfast. Although relieved they hadn't been caught, Eric knew they still had a long way to go before this was all over. But the first step to bringing an ending to the rather dark tale meant another trip to the Grizzlydale Public Library and the odd Mr. Gregory.

After lunch, they all piled into the car. There was no hiding the massive bruise that took up a large portion of the left side of Heather's nose. Earlina's concern was unmistakable.

"Oh, sweetie. What the heck happened to you? Is everything okay at home? What's going on?"

Heather was again taken back by Earlina's rather aggressive sense of compassion.

"Oh, it's nothing. I mean, it looks a lot worse than it feels.

Honest."

Earlina was having none of that.

"That's not what I asked, young lady. Now, if there is a problem, you can tell me. I promise, we'll keep you safe."

Eric was doing his best to give his friend the sign for "stall" as he thought of something to tell his mom. However, as Heather was soon learning, there was no one more dedicated as Eric's mom when she felt one of her kids were in trouble. And something told Heather that by being Eric's only real friend, she had most definitely fallen into the realm of "Earlina's kid."

"Um, I was trying to. I was trying." Eric could tell his friend was faltering. While he knew neither of them wanted to tell his mom what really happened the night before, he also knew the truth just wasn't going to cut it. There was no way anyone could convince an adult that Heather's bruised nose was on account of her trying to run from what seemed to be her beloved pet possessed by an ancient and evil Native American mythological monster. Nope, that was not going to fly in any way. Eric stepped in.

"She tried to work on her bike and a piece broke off and hit her. It was really nasty, mom, you should have seen it."

Earlina looked closely at her son's friend. "Is that true?"

To her credit, Heather didn't pause in her reply.

"Yes ma'am. I mean, Earlina. It's just a little embarrassing." Eric, pressing the issue spoke up again.

"And that's why we're going to hit the library. Get the right information, so it doesn't happen again. Right?"

Heather nodded and smiled at Eric. "Right."

Earlina turned back to the dashboard of the car and turned

the key. As the engine came to life, she shook her head.

"I don't really know what I'm going to do with you two." And with that, they made their way to the library...

18
THE OTHER DOOR

A library that they learned, twenty minutes later, was closed. Or, at least that's what the sign on the main door proclaimed, backed up by the large "DO NOT CROSS" tape that zigzagged over the damaged cement steps leading up to the converted jail.

"Oh, great," proclaimed Eric as he jumped out from the car. Heather started to make her way out as well, concern starting to show on her face.

"Guys, there is no reason for you to get out. Come on, we can check again in a couple of days," said Eric's mom. Both Eric and Heather stood in disappointment outside the car, looking up at the rather silent-appearing library. Earlina gently tapped on the horn. "Come on, there's no point in standing around. Let's go. We'll pick up something fun for dinner later." Eric and Heather both slowly turned back to the car.

"Wait! Wait! We're open. Don't go!" The yelling came from behind the massive stone structure as the wild-haired librarian made his way to the front. "Ah! Stupid rumbling. It caused a few cracks in the steps, so the town council had me tape it off, for safety reasons."

Eric tilted his head. He still wasn't sure how to take Mr. Gregory after their last encounter. Heather, however, pointed at the turned CLOSED sign.

"Then why is that up?"

Mr. Gregory looked at the sign and shook his head in annoyance.

"Because, young lady, I am not the young man I once was and forgot to turn the sign back to open." He then turned back to Earlina. "You can leave them here if you wish, Mrs. Del Bosque. Eric was a joy to have around last time, and I am sure he and his friend have plenty of work they want to do."

Earlina waved at the librarian and thanked him. Then she looked back at Eric and Heather.

"Okay, you two. I will be back in an hour. Just one hour. Be ready this time, I mean it." Both Eric and Heather waved back and promised they'd be outside. And with that, Earlina drove down the road. Eric and Heather turned back to Mr. Gregory, who was already carrying a grin that made both of them feel a chill down their spine.

"I had a feeling I'd be seeing you both today." He turned and made a motion with his hand to follow him. "Come this way; we need to use the other door." Both Eric and Heather did as they were asked. Unable to contain herself, Heather spoke up.

"You mean the back door, right? The back door to the library?"

Mr. Gregory chuckled.

"Oh, no, Ms. Foster. I meant the other door." And with that, he rounded the corner and placed his right palm over a plain stone wall. With his left hand he gestured in the air a strange pattern that quickly molded into a green glowing symbol, just floating in the air. With that, Mr. Gregory traced a door-shaped arc on the stone wall with his right hand.

Eric gasped as he saw a faint green hue reveal itself where Mr. Gregory traced his left hand. Mr. Gregory turned to look at Eric and smiled.

"Ah, so you saw that. My suspicions were correct. I was hoping they were."

Eric took a few steps forward. Heather reached out and grabbed her friend by the arm. Mr. Gregory simply kept smiling.

"Your desire to protect your friend is quite admirable, Ms. Foster. But I assure you, I have no desire to harm Eric or you. Indeed, what we are about to do will protect you both on the path that events have set upon you."

Eric looked back at his friend and silently mouthed, "It's okay." Heather tilted her eyebrow a bit, and then relaxed her grip. With a gust of wind, a door opened where there was once a plain stone wall meant to hold Grizzlydale's worst from over a century ago. Mr. Gregory stepped inside.

"Well, don't just stand out there. You said you needed to use the library." Mr. Gregory smiled from within the opening and he motioned his hand towards the stairs that lead under the library. "It's time you discovered the true power within this building."

Slowly, Eric and Heather both went in.

"This isn't quite what I was expecting," whispered Heather

as the two friends moved deeper down the stairs.

If Mr. Gregory had heard her, he was doing his best to act otherwise. Eric nodded at his friend's comment and replied, "I know. I mean. Well, actually, I have no idea what we should have expected." Heather mumbled a reply that even Eric couldn't hear as they continued further still.

Finally, Mr. Gregory reached another unmarked door and reached into his pocket. Eric let out a slight gasp when he saw that the hand that entered Mr. Gregory's pocket was not the hand that came out. Sure, it was still connected to the librarian. But what was once a healthy, if slightly older hand, was now a tattered collection of dried skin and bone. Heather, never one to act or speak with any form of subtlety, did nothing to hide her concern.

"Whoa! You expect me and Eric to follow the mummy into his special kill room?" Heather grabbed onto Eric forcefully and continued, "No way. Eric, let's get the heck out of here. I don't know what we were thinking!"

Eric didn't fight his friend; although not as vocal, his feelings on the situation were the same. Mr. Gregory didn't turn around. He simply inserted the key his skeletal hand had removed from his pocket into the keyhole and unlatched the lock. The room filled with a green glow as torches that neither Eric or Heather had first seen upon entering illuminated the room. Still without turning, Mr. Gregory pushed open the door and spoke.

"I am sorry, Eric. I should have told you the truth earlier. But now, now there is little time for pleasantries." And with that, Mr. Gregory started to move through the open door, still ignoring the two children that were moving with all speed back the way they came in and back outside.

"Is he trying to catch us?" asked Heather as she pulled Eric along the way. Eric took a second to turn his head back.

"No, he just went into some other room. Oh, man, Heather, what did I get us into?"

"Don't know. Don't care. We're getting out of here." Reaching the entrance she flung open the door they had just passed through mere minutes before. As the outside light shined a reddish hue upon her face, Heather again let out a colorful phrase that would earn Eric a night without dinner had he even started to speak the words. As Eric looked up with this friend, he understood her reason for saying it.

"Where did the town go?"

Outside, he and Heather saw a sight that looked familiar, yet was utterly and completely foreign. They took a few more steps, and while they were still within the confines or at least the general area of the Grizzlydale Public Library, it didn't look normal. The homes and courthouse that surrounded the building were nowhere to be seen. Only the large trees that all the kids of the town knew as the Hanging Oaks swayed in the eerily warm wind. On one of the large trees hung a rope, its threads digging deep into a branch, as if in time both would become one. In that moment, Eric understood what had happened. He looked up at the sky. Its reddish hue was not coming from a sunset or sunrise. It was the time of ash, when the volcano opened up and sent its fire and smoke into the skies, when the ground shook and the very first Tyrs opened. It was the day when Grizzlydale changed forever. Heather turned to Eric.

"Please tell me this isn't happening."

Eric could only shake his head.

"I think we shifted in time. The same thing happened to me when I went into the barn."

"But this isn't the barn, Eric. This is a whole building. We were in the building." Heather let out a cry as a horrible thought entered her mind: a memory of Eric's flashlight, forever trapped in stone. "No! Eric, what if this closes and we're here? No, I won't die like this. No! Eric, we have to make a run for it. We have to get out of here, now!" She started to pull his arm again. Eric did his best to let go, to try and convince Heather to slow down for just a moment, but she was simply too strong for him. From below, words gave them both a chance to pause.

"Please, you must come back inside. I promise, after you learn what I must tell you, you will return to your place and time."

Both looked back and saw the horrific sight of a Mr. Gregory that looked many, many decades dead. His visage was one of death and decay. And yet for all the fear that Eric should have been feeling, he saw something in Mr. Gregory's eyes. The body was dead, of that there was no doubt, but in those eyes Eric saw life. He saw hope and truth. "I swear to you both, no harm will come to you as long as I am here. But I can't follow you outside. If you leave and the Tyr closes, I cannot help."

Eric looked up at his friend. He could tell her instincts were still telling her to run. But it was a credit to their growing friendship that she didn't. For in the short time they'd become friends, Heather did trust Eric, and if he wasn't going to run, neither was she.

"I know this is a lot to take in. But I swear to you, if you stay here, in this time, everyone and everything you know will be lost forever." Mr. Gregory stretched his hands out further to Eric and Heather as he spoke the final words.

Heather glanced back at the red and foreign land she called home and then back to Eric. With a small nod and weak grin to Eric, they both made their way down the stairs, back toward the library and to the living dead man they called Mr. Gregory.

Inside, the green light had a calming effect on both Eric and Heather. As if all this craziness would somehow start to make sense, Mr. Gregory replied in kind.

"I imagine you'd like some explanation."

Eric again wondered if his mind was some blank slate that just any person could read. He shook the thought away as paranoia that was only going to get him in trouble one day.

"Oh no, Eric Del Bosque. That paranoia will most definitely save you; just don't let it rule your life."

Eric and Heather stopped dead in their tracks as Mr. Gregory let out a dusty laugh that would almost sound comical, where they not lost in space and time. "Don't worry, young man. Most people, even most creatures, can't read your mind. It's something special I picked up once I took this form. To be perfectly honest, it surprised and frightened the heck out of me the first time."

This time Heather stepped up and asked the most obvious of questions, as Eric was still lost in his own mind following this revelation.

"Just what are you? I mean, you can't really be Grizzlydale's librarian."

"I most definitely am the librarian. In fact, I am Grizzlydale's only librarian. Since day one." The three of them had again reached the door that first caused the lights to change and the shift in time. "Although I will admit that was not my goal when I first accepted this position over a hundred years ago." He stepped aside and with some fanfare, presented the open doorway. "Please, after you. I promise the room is quite safe. Far safer than lingering outside."

Both Eric and Heather moved to the door with little hesitation. It came as quite the shock to both of them how the bizarre was becoming normal. As they passed Mr. Gregory, he turned his head to Heather and smiled. Not with any malice or deceit. More like an approving parent, or a proud teacher. After they were fully in the room, Mr. Gregory followed.

The room was quite orderly. More like a small office, at home anywhere. In the middle of the room sat a desk with a couple of chairs on both sides. Some paintings and even a few tattered photographs lined the walls. In one corner, a couch with a decades-thick layer of dust sat utterly unattended. No matter how tired one was, that couch did not look like the most inviting place to rest. Against the far wall stood a massive wardrobe, sealed tight with chains and an incredibly sturdy-looking lock. Before Eric could speak or think, Mr. Gregory responded.

"Trust me. Not something you want to know about. At least not yet. Let us just focus on the task at hand." Mr. Gregory motioned for both kids to sit at his desk. They did so with little waiting.

"When you first came here, Eric, I was curious why you wanted to know the history of this town. It's not a subject most kids care to know about, at least not without a teacher assigning it."

Eric nodded.

"I was more than happy to show you some of the books and go along with my day. Then you asked about the volcano. More specifically, the year between the time before and after the eruption. That, my friend, had me hooked."

Heather let out a small grunt.

"So what's the big deal. Eric's a book nerd; he's always reading. Even when we hang out, he's got a book on him."

Eric made a look of mock hurt feelings.

"Hey! I'm not that bad."

"Yes, you are. It's okay, we're still buddies."

They had a small laugh together and abruptly stopped when they saw that Mr. Gregory seemed less than amused. The awkward moment passed as he smiled.

"Your camaraderie is good. You'll need it." Reaching to open a drawer in the desk, Mr. Gregory continued. "As you say, Ms. Foster, being curious about history isn't all that odd, even for a child." Mr. Gregory pulled a sealed leather tube from the desk and set it on the desk. Eric noticed some of the same symbols that had been on the clothes Tocho wore. "However, the very fact that Eric asked about a specific year was odd."

Heather was still unconvinced and her questioning face proved it. The undead librarian let our a dusty sigh. "Young lady, can you tell me the year Grizzlydale was founded?"

Heather grinned.

"Of course, every kid knows that. It was in June..." She smiled wider still as Mr. Gregory looked at her with

THE OTHER DOOR 197

approval.

Eric looked at his friend in confusion.

"Wait, I didn't hear her say the year."

Heather looked at Eric and rolled her eyes.

"Oh, now you want to play the creepy part like mister mummy over here?"

Mr. Gregory leaned closer to the kids.

"Please, Heather, humor your friend. Tell him again when Grizzlydale formed as a town."

Heather sighed.

"Fine. One more time, June... Happy?"

Eric looked at Mr. Gregory.

"But she still didn't say the year." Heather threw her arms in the air, annoyed with both of them.

Mr. Gregory responded.

"She did. At least she thinks she did. Tell me, young lady, were you born in Grizzlydale?"

"Ugh, yes, unfortunately."

Mr. Gregory again smiled.

"Behold the gift and curse that is the Tyrs of Grizzlydale. No child of the town, or anyone that spends a long time here, can remember a time when there wasn't a Grizzlydale. Sure, they think they know. They'll even try and tell you the exact year, just as your friend attempted. But, they do not know. When that volcano erupted, the ground shook and broke open. It caused the first Tyrs to open. The very fabric of space, time, and reality burst forth. The town we all call home was changed, forever."

Heather wasn't buying it.

"This is stupid. I just told you the year the town formed. I know it. Everyone knows it. Quite messing with me and Eric. Just stop!"

Mr. Gregory raised his palms in a calming gesture.

"Please. I am not trying to upset you. I know you truly believe what you just said. Because, to you it is true. Utterly and completely. Such is the effect the Tyrs have on everyone that lives in this town."

This time it was Eric who spoke up.

"Then why was I able to learn the real year? Why wasn't I affected by these Tyrs? I mean, I wasn't born here, but I've been in this town for most of my life. I don't even remember moving here, I was so young. Still, I know I am not from Grizzlydale."

Mr. Gregory sat back and stroked what was left of his chin. Both Eric and Heather made no attempt to hide their disgust as bits of crispy skin and maybe even a bone chip fell off and onto the floor. "Ah, sorry about that. I often forget that you can see my true nature."

"Yeah," chimed in Heather. "About that."

"I fell into a Tyr fissure the moment the ground shook. As best as I can tell, as long as energy from the Tyrs continues to influence and affect this town, I will not die. Though as you see, I still age."

Ever curious, Eric pressed further.

"Then why do you look normal, like, everywhere else?"

Mr. Gregory pondered for a moment and then leaned back in his chair.

"You aren't going to like the answer."

Heather countered, "I don't like any of this."

"The truth, then." Mr. Gregory leaned back in his chair,

his gaze shifting to the floor and ceiling, as if in deep thought, pondering his reply. "The truth is," he smiled, "that I have no idea."

Heather jumped from her chair.

"Great! We get clueless Yoda."

Mr. Gregory continued, ignoring the rather annoyed Heather Foster.

"Sadly, I also don't know why you weren't affected by long-term exposure to Tyr energy, Eric. Still, I am convinced that you are somehow connected to the land. To the Tyrs themselves. Even now, I can see an aura around you that tells me you've freely entered and left one."

Eric nodded.

"Well, wasn't all that freely. We were looking for Heather's lost dog. A lot of missing pets, really. Everyone thinks it's just wild animals taking them. But, I've been reading this book. It talks about an ancient spirit. An evil spirit that takes control of all the beasts of the land. And I'm pretty sure I live next to its lair."

Mr. Gregory didn't miss a beat.

"Ah, yes, the Hairy Baby. Although that's not what it was called when these events first happened."

Without letting Mr. Gregory finish, Heather cut him off.

"Wait. I realize that I should be getting used to weird things, what with the lord of the dead standing before us."

Eric chuckled, "I think he's technically undead." Even the librarian couldn't stifle a small laugh, a laugh that sent some dust and other matter into the air.

Heather continued.

"Okay, first, Eric, not helping. Second, it doesn't matter.

And third, just how the heck do you know about Hairy Baby? I never once saw you in Ashen Forest Estates, and I am pretty sure no one else has either. In fact, I've don't remember ever seeing you outside this stupid library. So come on now. Speak, or hack, or whatever you do."

Mr. Gregory sat patiently. Heather grew more annoyed. "Well?"

The undead librarian grinned anew.

"Sorry. I was making sure you were completely finished before I continued my thought." Mr. Gregory looked at both kids, their attention fully locked on him.

"Very well. As you so subtly pointed out, Ms. Foster, no, I have never lived on the mountain. Indeed, since the time of the volcano's first eruption, I have been trapped within the Tyr lines of this very spot. However, as I was saying, the creature that now stirs was not always contained to your home. There was a dark period in history, no matter how short, where it was free to cause death and horrors to all that called this region home. Although I assure you, in those days, it did not have such a innocuous name." He looked deeply at the two kids, both of whom were enchanted by his words. "In those times, we called it—"

Eric cut him off. "The Hemei Ninambebea."

Mr. Gregory's eyes grew wide. "Ah, then you did see her. You saw the child Tocho."

Heather sat back down, her curiosity overcoming her annoyance. This was something she wanted to hear as well, though for reasons both she and Eric would not understand for a very long time.

"Well, I wouldn't call her a child. I mean, I guess she was

young, but she looked older than you, Heather," said Eric. Heather simply grunted and folded her arms. Eric had no idea why, but she looked annoyed with him. "But yes, I saw her. She told me about the Hemei Ninambebea, and how she and some people from her village and the town went to confront it. It worked. That is, until my family moved in and, um, well, cracked his cage. I guess."

Mr. Gregory nodded and slid the leather tube towards Eric.

"I think I am beginning to understand. While it doesn't fully explain why your memory of the town is so complete, I think your connection to the Tyrs goes far deeper than simply being near one. For better or worse, young Eric Del Bosque, you are now Tyr-touched. You are as much a part of the land as I, and those rare few that have Tyr energy flow through them."

Heather looked at Mr. Gregory with disgust.

"Ew, does that mean Eric is going to turn all zombie and stuff?"

Mr. Gregory laughed.

"I think not, young lady. The Tyrs affect everyone differently. They even affect you."

Heather shook her head.

"Nu-uh. No way. I'm not some freak. And I know when the town was founded, dang it!"

"Indeed. Please, think of something to tell me. In fact, why do you both try and think of something in your mind? But, Ms. Foster, try not to use your colorful vocabulary, as anyone can imagine that."

Both Eric and Heather squinted their eyes, clearly trying

to think of something wholly bizarre. After a few seconds, they looked directly at Mr. Gregory.

Grizzlydale's oldest and apparently only librarian first turned his gaze to Eric, smiling and nodding his head. "I assure you, young man, we will be finished here long before your mom pulls up. There will be no need for us to think of a excuse about this entire meeting." Eric's eyes shot open; Heather merely rolled hers.

"Really, Eric? That was the best you could do? Even I could guess you're worried about getting in trouble. That's all you think about, when you aren't convincing me to save the world, or something." She turned back to Mr. Gregory. "Well, what you got on me, Jacob Marley?"

Again, Mr. Gregory focused on the young girl before him. He stared at her for a long time, so long that both Heather and Eric began to squirm in discomfort. Finally, Gregory shook his head and spoke.

"I sense nothing."

Heather laughed.

"Ha! I was thinking about how I'd really love some pizza right now. Deep dish. With extra mushrooms, and some sausage, and then more mushrooms. Loser."

Again, Mr. Gregory smiled.

"Then it is as I thought. You have indeed been touched by the Tyrs."

Heather countered,

"No, I'm just not as simple as my buddy over here. Just admit it."

Mr. Gregory countered.

"You miss my point, child. It wasn't that I read you wrong.

I could not read you. In fact, were it not physically evident that you are in this room, I would not know you existed at all. You are, for lack of a better term, psychically invisible. And that, my dear, is a very strange and special gift."

Heather shook her head.

"No, now you're just messing with me, with both of us. Right, Eric?"

Eric sat there, very still, looking dumbfounded at his friend. Mr. Gregory, sensing a moment to affirm his findings to both, spoke again as to Eric's thoughts. "You're right, young man; that many mushrooms on pizza is strange." He turned back to Heather and continued. "You will make a valuable ally in the coming days." Eric looked at his friend and shrugged. Heather was not so silent.

"Ally? No, I just want to find my pet and have a normal summer. That's what Eric and I both want. Right?"

Eric nodded back. "Yeah, I'd be happy with that."

Mr. Gregory shook his head.

"I am afraid that choice has passed. You are both part of a larger story that started over a hundred years ago. For good or ill, it's a story that needs its final chapters written." With that, he reached over and placed the leather tube into Eric's hands.

"Now, if I remember correctly, your mother is about to pick you both up soon. I think it's time we went back outside and waited for her."

He got up and made his way to the door. Both Eric and Heather sat still for a moment before they rose together and followed him. Heather broke the awkward silence.

"You think Rusty and Spit have their own crazy undead

guy that tells them they're some special gate people and gives them weird tasks about saving the town?"

Eric looked at her and smirked. "Nope, I don't either."

For all her posing, Eric was glad to have a friend like Heather. No matter how strange things got, she always had a smile or a quip to keep them both grounded. He just hoped he was as good a friend in return.

Outside the room Mr. Gregory again turned the key and unlocked the door. The green-hued torches went out and the exterior door opened to reveal the bright summer sun they had left a little under an hour before. Mr. Gregory started to make his way outside.

"Whoa! You can't let my mom see you like that!" Eric panicked as he saw Earlina as she pulled up in the car. Mr. Gregory turned back to Eric and, wearing a smile that was 100% alive, winked at him.

"I don't know what you are talking about, young man."

Both Eric and Heather tried to hide the shock on their faces. This whole Tyr stuff and time jumping was never going to get easy.

Eric's mom waved at the three of them.

"Right on time. Well done!"

Eric and Heather made their way towards the car. Mr. Gregory patted Eric on the back.

"Always good to see kids so eager to learn. Come back anytime." They started to open the doors when Mr. Gregory again stopped them. "Wait—you almost forgot the book you checked out." He handed Heather a copy of The Fool's Guide to Bike Repair. As he did so, he leaned in toward the two kids.

"Remember what I said. Read what's in that case. Finish the story." Standing tall, he smiled at Earlina and bade them a good day.

The kids buckled themselves in for the ride back up the mountain. Unable to contain his curiosity, Eric quietly opened the leather tube. Inside were slips of paper. Horrific images of what he could only assume was the Hemei Ninambebea in its various forms greeted him. Along with the images were words and notes on just how the beast could be stopped once and for all. He leaned over to his friend.

"Um, we're gonna need some help on this one."

As they went back up the mountain, the rumble of the large car masked the slight shaking of the ground. And had they looked up from the papers Mr. Gregory gave them, both Eric and Heather would have seen the small plume of smoke coming from Mt. Ashen.

Their home.

19
MAKING PLANS

Eric felt a twinge of guilt as he cleared the table after breakfast. Although he had been known to stretch the truth from time to time with his parents in order to avoid trouble, the events of the past few weeks were different. This was serious and part of him felt he should at least give them an idea of what he and Heather had learned. Eric set some plates into the sink and turned on the faucet and began the nightly task of cleaning the dishes before placing them in the dishwasher. To this day, he never understood why. Not realizing he'd let out yet another sigh as he scrubbed, his mom chimed in.

"Because the dishwasher is for sanitizing them, not for getting off all the big chunks."

Eric didn't reply. This was a conversational battle which only his mother would win. His dad, however, could never resist the challenge.

"You know, by definition, a dishwasher does just that. Washes dishes. As in the whole dish and everything on it."

"No, it makes them extra clean. I'm sorry, but my mom and her mom before her washed all their dishes before putting them in the machine. And let me tell you, not a single member of our family ever got sick from dirty dishes."

"No one gets sick from dirty dishes."

"You're right—not in this house!"

"Wait, you said your grandmother didn't even have a dishwasher until she moved to America."

Even with his back turned, Eric could feel his mom grin and know that his father's logic was soon about to face the immovable object that was Earlina and her patented That's right.

And then, right on cue.

"That's right."

A silence followed her statement. There was really little anyone could do once his mom dropped that line. It was a rather humorous way to suggest that the conversation was over and for everyone's sake, perhaps they should move on to another topic. Eric opened the dishwasher to add the now-pristine dishes to their next stage of hyper-vigilant cleanliness. His dad also took the hint.

"Did you hear that some animal, or animals, killed more cows at the Craftgrower's ranch?"

Eric stiffened a bit as he heard his dad ask the question. Although farming and ranch life was about as far away from his dad's profession as one could imagine, you couldn't live in Grizzlydale without calling one or two farmers your friend.

Earlina replied, "I knew about the carcasses they found last week, but I hadn't heard of anything new."

Eric's dad continued.

"Yup, I found out on my way home when I stopped off for some gas. Tommy Craftgrower found them this morning when he realized his head count was off. By a lot."

"How many?"

"At least seven cattle, but a few more are still missing. He's already assuming they're gone as well."

Earlina let out a whistle of shock. "That's a lot of money to just lose."

"Almost nine thousand dollars. Probably more, since he said a couple more were pretty beat up. He can sell them for meat, but he's lost any breeding potential."

"Does anyone have any idea what's going on? I mean, lots of families up here are missing pets. There is no way that's not connected somehow."

"Beats me. Just glad we didn't get a dog like we originally planned when we moved up here."

To that, Eric finally stepped into the conversation.

"Wait. We were going to get a dog?"

His dad turned to face him.

"It was going to be a surprise, later in the summer, once we got the house settled a bit more."

His mom then joined in. "But, mijo, with all the missing pets, even your friend Heather's dog. Maybe we should wait and see what's going on. You wouldn't want whatever you picked to get hurt. Would you?"

Eric was a little saddened, but he did agree with his parents. And, it was awfully nice of them to want to surprise him. Eric had always wanted a dog. A big one, like the Dire Wolves he always read about in his fantasy books, or at least the closest a kid in rural America could come to such a creature.

"No, that's probably a good idea."

"That does remind me," his mom continued. "Has Heather heard anything about her dog"?

Eric shook his head.

"No. I think she's ready to give up. It sucks."

"Eric, watch the language."

"Sorry."

"Although the boy isn't wrong," his dad added. "No one ever wants to lose a pet. But to never know what happened—hmm, that's a shame."

Eric looked at his dad and smiled. Although they didn't spend as much time together as Eric (or his mom) had wanted, he was the kind of dad that at least had his back when it came to stuff at home. It was a strange relationship and one that Eric wanted to do more about—once he was done putting an ancient, animal-possessing spirit of evil to rest, that is. No big deal. Breaking the sad silence, Eric said,

"Speaking of Heather. Do you mind if I pop over there and hang out?"

His dad shrugged, the universal dad sign for "I don't care," while his mom thought a bit more, as she always did, before answering.

"If it's okay with her mom, sure."

"Um, I don't think her mom is home right now. At least I don't see her car over there."

"Then how do you know Heather is home?"

"I already saw her outside, watering the, the... Um, watering the cars actually."

His dad raised an eyebrow. "Watering the cars?"

"She keeps some flowers in the trunks of a couple of the trashed ones. She says it's her Arma-Carden-Garden." Eric smiled; even he thought it was a great name.

His dad merely shook his head.

"Of course this is a person you make friends with."

Earlina however, was not as amused.

"You know how I feel about you being over there when no one is home."

His dad rolled his eyes a bit.

"Really, Earlina? The boy is eleven years old and about as interested in girls as, well, an eleven-year-old boy. I think you can relax."

This time is was Eric's mom that looked a little flushed.

"Now, that's not what I meant. I mean—Darn it, Franco. Fine, go ahead, but check in every couple of hours. And if you guys want, I can make you lunch later."

Eric smiled.

"Thanks, mom, dad.". With more than a little excitement, he ran to his room to grab a few things. As he did so, he wondered just what his mom and dad meant by being eleven over at Heather's house. He figured his dad was right, because whatever his mom's concern, he was indeed oblivious. Grabbing his backpack, he shoved The Tale of Tocho and the leather case inside and made his way outside and to Heather's house.

He knocked on the door, and after a few moments and another colorful phrase that made him smile and blush a little, his friend swung open the door.

"What took you so long?"

Eric walked in and set his backpack on the couch.

MAKING PLANS

"I had to do the dishes."

"You guys own a dishwasher. I've seen it."

"Trust me, you don't want the whole story."

Heather stood with the door open and looked at her friend, then smiled.

"Nope. I don't." After walking into her kitchen, she opened the refrigerator and pulled out a packaged snack box. "You want one?"

Eric shook his head.

"No, I just ate. How can you still be hungry just after breakfast?"

"What are you talking about? This is breakfast for me."

"Oh, so I guess you and your mom didn't, um." He stopped himself, realizing he was again assuming everyone had a home that he was learning he was quite lucky to have. To her credit, Heather simply smiled as she popped some kind of meat and cheese thing in her mouth.

"Oh, I guarantee whatever these things are made from is still better for me than whatever my mom would make." For a brief moment Eric thought about asking just what her mom did, and why she was rarely around. Wisely, he decided that was a conversation for another day.

"Fair enough," he replied as he opened the backpack. "So, we've got a lot of work to do."

Heather nodded as she plopped herself on a very worn lounge chair.

"Yeah, I've been thinking about what you said on the drive home yesterday. And I think you're right. We're going to need help on this one."

"Yes, we are, so how do we going about convincing our

parents that all these animal disappearances and attacks are the work of the Hairy Baby?"

Heather popped a couple more food items in her mouth. She started to talk but noticed that most of what she put in was falling back out. Embarrassed, she covered her mouth with one hand and raised the other letting Eric know that she was going to need a few seconds. After a less than dignified gulp, she continued.

"Whew, that was a bit much. Anyway, yeah, I've been thinking on that."

"And?"

"And here's the thing. Being pulled into strange time and space notwithstanding, you and I have done pretty well so far."

"That's true, but we got lucky last time. I mean, if I hadn't learned those words from Tocho, who knows what Hoss would have done to me, to you." As soon as the words left his mouth, Eric knew he had pushed a little too hard. Heather pulled her gangly legs up and onto the chair. Grabbing ankles with her hands, she tightened up as the memory of seeing her beloved dog altered in such a way that she barely recognized him was almost too much for her.

"I'm sorry. I didn't mean to say it like that."

Heather pulled back a sniffle and nodded.

"I know. And I'm not mad at you, honest. It's just, Hoss was always the one thing, person, I could rely on. He was there for everything."

"You know there is still a chance we can get him back. I mean, nothing in the pages I've read from the leather case say anything about losing the animal. That is, if we can get to

Hoss before the possession is complete."

"Thanks for trying to help, Eric, but I need to face reality. Or, as close to reality as my life's become since meeting you. My buddy is gone. Long gone."

This time it was Eric's turn to lower his head. For a while now he'd been wondering just what would have happened had he never gone into the barn that first day. Had he just put down the book his teacher gave him. It wasn't even that good of a story. Why he kept reading it, Eric did not know. There was no getting around the facts. One way or another, all this was his fault.

Heather noticed almost immediately that what she said had hurt her friend.

"Wait, Eric. That's not what I meant. I'm glad you and I met. You really are one of my best, or only, friends in this stupid neighborhood. And, as I am learning, it was only a matter of time before the, shoot, what's its real name again? Hemmy Nano, Himmee Ninabeees?"

"Hemei Ninambebea."

"Right, before Hairy Baby would have oozed its way out and into our world."

"But if I hadn't..."

"Hadn't what? Moved up here with your parents, without absolutely no say or control in the matter?" Heather stood up, clearly feeling moved by her own words. "We're just kids, Eric. There isn't a whole lot we can do when it comes to parents." She paused a moment, a hint of anger rising in her voice. "Or our moms." Eric looked up at his friend and saw the same tough girl that pulled him off the ground all those weeks ago. "But what we can take care of is this you-know-what of a monster that's turning our pets into monsters and put it down. For good!"

Eric couldn't stop himself; he leapt to his feet with a cheer and raised a palm to the air, a few feet from Heather's face.

"What are you doing?"

Eric kept up his weird smile.

"Um, a high-five?"

Heather was not able to contain her laughter as she fell back to the lounge chair.

"Eric, you are, without a doubt, the dorkiest person I have ever met." Eric smiled and with a hint of defeat, lowered his hand. "But I am also so very glad we're friends."

"Me too," he replied. "Now then, about getting some help and convincing our families about what's going on. I think I can put together a presentation with all the information we have and—"

Heather cut him off.

"Have you listened to anything I just said?" She pointed at the couch. Eric understood and sat back down. "Adults aren't going to help. They're just going to tell us we're a couple of stupid kids with too much free time, and probably tell us we can't hang out anymore."

Eric looked at his friend, rather dumbfounded.

"Then what's your idea?"

Heather leaned back in her chair, took a deep breath, rubbed her face, and let out an incredibly drawn-out exhale.

"You are not going to like it."

"Like what?"

"So, to do this, we need people that know Ashen Forest Estates better than anyone. Someone that's just nasty enough to not run and isn't afraid to fight dirty while you do whatever it is you're supposed to do with all those papers and notes."

"Yeah, I'm still working on that part."

Heather shook her head.

"That does not fill me with confidence, Eric."

"I'm working on it. Trust me."

"Fine." She learned forward, as if what she was going to say next would mean the difference between life and death.

"There is only one person I can think of that fits what we need."

Eric leaned forward as well.

"And that person is?"

Heather smiled.

"Rusty."

Eric leapt from the couch and started spewing a stream of words that would have kept him grounded to his room until he graduated college, assuming of course such words allowed him to even live that long after the wrath of a furious mother had its way with him.

Heather, however, leaned back and smiled.

"Exactly."

20
WITH FRIENDS LIKE THESE

"You know it would be a lot easier if you just let me pedal us up to Rusty's house."

Eric promptly put the brakes on his bike upon hearing Heather comment yet again on his rather slow pace.

"Listen, it's bad enough that you talked me into this plan. I mean, getting Rusty and his nasty toad of a sidekick to help us is one thing. But, if you expect me to face those two while holding onto you, well..."

Heather leaned over her much shorter friend's shoulder and said, "Well, what?"

"Well, I don't know. Just trust me. It's a bad idea. A bad idea piled on top of what is probably going to get us beat to a black and blue pulp anyway."

"So? We're just trying to talk them into helping us get killed by some horrible creature anyway."

"True, but at least when Hairy Baby takes us, it will be swift. The red-headed tyrant of Ashen Forest Estates will take his sweet time with us, and who knows what Spit will do once Rusty gets bored."

"Come on, it won't be that bad. Although at the rate you're riding, this will all be over before we get there. Just let me take over, Eric."

"No. Not going to happen. I'm not going to let a girl—" And with that, Eric felt his burden grow eighty-five pounds lighter as Heather jumped off the back.

"You did not just pull the 'by a girl' crap on me!"

Eric let out a big sigh and got off the bike. He gently set the bike down and turned to his friend, who was quite the image of red anger.

Heather cut loose. "You know you set your bike down like a girl, right?"

Eric stuffed his hands in his pockets. This was going well.

"You know that's not what I meant."

"No, I don't know. So, educate me, mister big brain book guy that couldn't even pull his butt off the dirt without whimpering the first time I met him."

There were only a few moments in Eric's life where he wished he could take back something that he'd said. This moment here, without a doubt, had just shot up to first place and he couldn't think of anything else that would ever replace it. In the short time he called Heather his friend, he had learned that she was one of the most independent and fierce kids in Ashen Estates. They never talked about it, but having a parent that was rarely around and being the only girl in an area of rather rough boys made her someone that worked extra hard at proving herself. He was going to have to tread lightly if he wanted to get out of this with a friend.

"Heather. You know there are so many things I do that

you do about a hundred times better."

"There are about a hundred things I do that you can't even attempt. Like reach the top shelf."

"Okay, I deserved that one."

"You're darn right you did."

"What I mean is, Rusty is like a wild animal. Probably not all the different than the creature we're trying to put away for good."

"And that means you can pull the same stuff everyone has pulled on me since I can remember?"

"No, of course it doesn't. And that's not how I meant it. Please, just listen."

"Fine."

"Convincing Rusty to not take his revenge on us immediately, let alone help us out, is going to be hard enough when he sees me."

"Still wondering where your idiotic dig on me being a girl comes into all this."

"Like I said, we need to treat Rusty like a big mean dog. That kind only responds to authority and strength."

"Of which you have none."

"Okay, stop! I know I just made you mad, but you really need to hear me out on this."

Heather glared at her friend. Maybe this wasn't going to be enough to end their friendship, but there was definitely a look of hurt behind the anger, hurt that Eric realized his friend had felt far too many times in her thirteen years on this planet.

"It's a simple as this. If he sees you riding, with me on the back of the bike, all he's going to do is laugh. Laugh, and then come after us. It's stupid, but I know how bullies like him are wired. Trust me, I've been on the receiving end far too many times."

"And if he sees you huffing and puffing while I hang on?"

"He'll still want to pound us, but he'll at least be curious why we're there."

Heather uncrossed her arms, while there was still anger and hurt behind her eyes, her pose softened just a bit.

"Boys make no sense."

"None at all." Eric smiled, picked his bike back up and held it still. "Please?"

Heather stood there for a few moments longer. Shaking her head, she walked back to Eric. He smiled back and hopped on the seat. A few seconds later Heather jumped on the riding bars behind him. She squeezed his shoulders a little harder than he liked and felt her breath in his ear.

"I'm sorry I got so mad. You've been the only person that never made me feel different. So when you said that—well, I guess the old Heather came out."

Eric turned his head to face his friend. He'd never seen her face this close before. It was strange, but not wholly unpleasing.

"I never meant to hurt you. Just because I read a lot doesn't mean I know all the right words. You have nothing to apologize for." And like that, Heather leaned back with a smile and released her grip enough to hold on but not bruise.

"So, shall we go get our butts kicked before hunting a Native American Volcano Dimensional Demon thing?"

Eric nodded.

"Yup, sounds good."

And with that, they continued their ride up to Rusty's house. Just as Heather predicted, the effort left Eric winded and wheezing. Also known as the dinner bell for bullies the world over.

Rusty's nasty little partner was the first to notice Eric and Heather ride to the edge of what they assumed was Rusty's house.

"Ay, Rusty, it's Stork and her nerd boyfriend!"

Heather hopped off the back of the bike and leaned in toward Eric.

"This is a perfect start".

Eric set his bike down.

"Stork?" he asked her quietly.

"I'll explain later. Ugh, I hate these guys." Eric and Heather saw that the bullies were making their way over to them. Eric noticed that Rusty had not put down the bat he was using to hit a tree, a tree that had clearly given him the stink eye. As they grew closer, Eric reminded Heather that this was her idea to begin with. She didn't have time to respond before a rock flew dangerously close to her head as they both heard Spit's rather cloying laugh.

Rusty leaned the baseball bat over his shoulder.

"Don't see your momma here, new kid."

"Eric. My name is Eric."

"Didn't ask."

Spit echoed his master in kind.

"Yeah, didn't ask."

Rusty shot his friend, if that's what they called each other, a dirty look. Eric smiled slightly; this was an interesting bit of knowledge.

"What's so funny, grease stain?"

Eric responded in the calmest voice he could muster.

"Nothing."

"No. Not nothing. You thought something was funny, so why don't you let me in on the joke."

Heather, not known for her subtlety, had no problem feeding Rusty's short temper.

"He could tell you, but you wouldn't get it. You know, brains and all."

"You know, Stork, I'm glad you started hanging out with this short loser. Saved me all the trouble of kicking you to the curb anyway. Skinny freckled freak. Seen your dad lately?"

Eric saw the anger swell up in his friend. In the time he'd gotten to know Heather, she had never once mentioned her dad, and seeing how even talking about her home life got her down, he felt it was best not to talk about it until she brought it up. So far, that had not happened. She let out a yell that actually made both Eric and Spit jump a bit as she charged full speed at Rusty.

"Heather! Wait. Don't, we need to—" But it was too late. What Rusty said had triggered something in Heather that Eric had never seen before. The few times he'd annoyed her, he thought he'd seen her at her angriest. This was something else. This felt almost dangerous. Her arm pulled back to deliver a nasty running punch. Eric knew he wasn't going to get through to her. He only hoped Rusty had enough humanity in him to not use the bat on his only friend.

For an instant, Eric thought his worst fears were coming to light as Rusty lifted the baseball bat from his shoulder. Heather was only a few feet away from Rusty when he stepped aside and simply stuck out his leg. Unable to stop herself, Heather tripped over his foot and went tumbling onto the hard dirt ground. She turned back to Rusty, his bat now pointed at her. Tears streamed down her face as she started screaming at Rusty with words that were far more colorful or profane than anything Eric had ever heard before. Although he was worried about the next few moments, Eric made a mental promise to himself to ask Heather just what had happened with her dad, in a time and place where she could stay calm. Rusty just stood there and laughed. A few people stuck their heads out their windows or doors. But this was Ashen Forest Estates; kids played rough up here, and as long as no one broke a bone or screamed bloody murder, the order of the day was "kids will be kids."

Spit, however, started making his way to Heather, with an extra-nasty look in his eye and another rock in his hand. Eric understood what that meant. As the lackey, Spit was always going to look for a way to impress his so-called friend. In a way, Eric found Spit far more deplorable than Rusty. Rusty was nasty to the bone, but something probably made him that way, something that, maybe someday, under the right guidance, he would grow out of. But people like Spit were mean and nasty because they liked it. And it was only his smaller stature that prevented him from calling the shots between the two.

"This isn't what I wanted," was all Eric could muster as he quickly moved behind Spit and grabbed his arm.

Spit turned and struggled to get free from Eric's grip. While it was true that Eric wasn't the strongest kid in the neighborhood (not even close), he had picked up a few skills from his dad and from the books he read. The commotion turned Rusty's attention from Heather. Both Eric and Spit started to struggle. Heather gathered herself while Rusty simply laughed and goaded his sidekick on.

"Come on! You gonna let this dork do that to you? I swear Spit, you let this nerd take you down and I'll help him beat you."

Eric was barely paying attention to Rusty's words, but he noticed the effect they were having on Spit. Still, he cursed himself for getting lost in the moment as Spit swung his free hand, the one holding the rock, and caught Eric square on the side of his head.

"Ah!" flew from Eric's mouth as the sky spun around him. He saw little bright spots appear at the sides of his vision as he felt his legs start to give out from under him. He heard Heather scream his name as he went down.

Yet somehow, against all odds, Eric kept his grip firm on his combatant. They both hit the ground hard. Eric again felt a sharp pain in his gut as Spit commenced jamming his knee against anything he could make contact with. Out of the corner of his eye, Eric saw Heather try and move in to help him, only for Rusty to wrap his arms around her waist and arms. She did her best to break free, but it was no use.

In a tone that sent a chill down what was left of Eric's spine, Rusty said, "Oh, yeah, new kid is gonna get it good. Maybe next time you'll pick better friends. If there is a next time, Stork." Eric felt another knee land on his gut and what little air he had left go from his lungs.

In the midst of all the fighting, Eric swore he felt the ground rumble, just a bit. But he couldn't tell if it was an accurate feeling, or just his now rattled brain sensing phantom events. Again, a slight rumble, clearly not in his head, as Spit slowed his attack to look at Rusty in confusion. Rusty only had the moment on his mind and mumbled something about making Eric bleed.

Then a strange calm came over Eric. He started to remember moves his dad had taught him during their rare moments of bonding, remember the lessons he read about that first night in his books. With dedicated motion, Eric slid his steel grip from Spit's upper arm down to his wrist. Wrapping his hand over Spit's, Eric pressed in. He pressed harder and harder until Spit's hand started to fold in on itself and the nasty little bully let out a scream that sounded like someone stepped on a cat's tail. Through his own pain, Eric spoke softly, with an eerie calm, into Spit's ear.

"We're both going to stand up. Slowly. If you fight back at all, I will break it right off."

Eric knew what he was doing wouldn't actually cause Spit's hand to come off. In truth, he knew this wouldn't even break a bone. But he knew it hurt. It had a kind of pain Spit had never experienced in his cruel little life . Spit started to stand, with Eric in complete control. Rusty's eyes widened in shock, and then anger. As he raised the bat, Heather grabbed it from his hands. Instinctively, he raised a fist to strike her. Heather was already posed to deliver a powerful blow of her own.

"Ow! Ow! OOOOOOOWWWWW!" came an ear-shattering howl from Spit, loud enough that it stopped Rusty's fist and Heather's back swing.

Eric locked his eyes on Rusty.

"Stop now, or I break him."

"I swear, you little piece of—"

Spit let out another wail as Eric pressed harder.

"Now!"

Even Eric was a little surprised and frightened by the ease with which he was able to inflict pain. Thankfully, he took no pleasure in the moment. Rusty lowered his fist and took a less threatening stance. Eric didn't apply more pressure, nor did he ease up. He looked at Heather, who was still holding the bat as a weapon, and nodded.

She stepped next to Eric and the whimpering Spit, and spoke.

"We just wanted to talk. And believe it or not, we came here for your help."

Eric followed her up. "If I let him go, will you listen?"

Spit begged Eric to let go and Rusty to listen. Rusty stood before them, seething with anger, but seeing more eyes on him from the neighbors windows, he quickly calmed himself. It made Eric understand that he was much smarter, or at least savvy in a primal sense, than he let on. In a move Eric never expected, Rusty started to laugh.

"Of course! Just having some fun. You know how it goes."

Eric started to ease off on Spit. "Not really, but I think I'm learning."

Spit ran away as Eric let go. "I'm telling my parents! You guys are so dead. Dead!"

Rusty just laughed more. "He'll be back." He held out his hand, asking for his baseball bat. Heather, still red with anger shook her head. "Whatever, Stork," he responded.

"It's Heather Foster. Start using it."

Rusty didn't reply. Instead, he turned to Eric.

"So, what did you want to talk about? Hurry, because I still really want to kick your butts and it's only because I have an audience now that I'm not unloading on both of you." As he finished, the ground shook again.

Suddenly, the air filled with a deafening boom as windows shattered, car alarms started screaming, and wind burst through the forest. Stunned from the shocking event, Eric and Heather braced themselves on each other, while Rusty took to a knee to steady himself.

Windows shattered and brittle trees fell as a second earth-shattering boom filled the once-peaceful air of Ashen Forest Estates.

The warm and bright summer sun started to die out as an ash cloud filled the sky. Everything around them took on a sinister red hue as ash from the mountain from which their neighborhood took its name finally opened again. Eric looked at Rusty.

"That."

The three of them stood in the middle of the street. Adults started rushing to their cars, while others shuttered their doors and windows. A few shouted at the kids to run home, to hurry and not look back. Eric looked around. Piercing the red hue was something else, something he didn't think was possible anymore. Or at least, in this time. He pointed to the edge of Ashen Forest Estates, past the last home on the border.

"Heather, look."

She looked where Eric was pointing. "Please tell me that's not what I think it is?"

Eric nodded his head. "Yeah, sorry. I think it is."

Shaken by the event, Rusty chimed in. "I don't know what you idiots are talking about, but I'm getting the heck out of here!"

Eric turned to Rusty. "Please, we're going to need your help."

Falling back on his old ways, Rusty shoved Eric to the ground. "Help nothing! Forget you guys!" And with all speed, Rusty started making his way back to his house, yelling out for his mom and dad.

Eric got up with Heather's help. As he stood, he watched Rusty running towards his house. Seeing it at the same time, both Eric and Heather slipped out a word that they dare not repeat in front of an adult.

"That's the biggest Tyr I've ever seen," added Heather.

Eric nodded his head. "Yup, and that idiot is going to run right into it."

21
THE TYRS IN REALITY

Eric ran back to his bike and pulled his backpack off the handlebars, while Heather started sprinting toward Rusty.

"I can't believe I'm actually trying to save this jerk."

"Not just him," replied Eric, "we're trying to save everyone."

She tackled Rusty and both of them went flying. Rusty tried to hit her, but Heather was waiting for his hit and blocked it with ease. "Please, Rusty. Trust us, we're trying to help."

Rusty wasn't having it. He shoved her back and turned to his home again. "Mom! Dad! Help!" In response to his yelling, Heather and Eric saw two red-headed adults make their way from the house, large bags in hand and shouting for Rusty to hurry up.

Heather shouted too. "Rusty! Dang it, if you keep going that way, you'll be lost forever!"

"Get your hands off me, freak!"

Heather did her best to hold onto the stronger boy, but it

was only a matter of time before he broke free and kept moving. All the while, his parents yelled at Heather to leave their son alone. The ground rumbled again, so strongly that Rusty's parents fell from their porch as it gave out from under them. Rusty let out a cry just as Eric reached Heather and her struggling companion.

Eric pulled a slip of paper from the leather tube and started speaking in a language that no one had uttered in Ashen Forest Estates in over a hundred years. Then Eric placed his hands on Rusty's head.

"See."

Rusty finally got Heather to let go as another rumble toppled trees, and in the distance, he heard an explosion as one of the hundreds of propane tanks that provided heat and fire to the residents of Ashen Forest Estates went up like a bomb. Rusty let out a gasp as his eyes revealed to him the horrible image that had been presented to Eric and Heather as soon as the sky darkened with ash. Green rips in the very ground spewed forth energy and images that he would never find the words to process.

He turned to Eric.

"What did you do to me, you freak?!"

Eric stood still before him.

"I'm sorry. It was the only way I could get you to believe us. It's how he gets out. How he possesses our pets and animals."

"'He' who?"

Eric cleared his throat. This was it. Now or never. Rusty would either help them or run to his screaming parents.

"The Hairy Baby."

Rusty's eyes seemed to double in size as he took in the horror of the neighborhood legend come to life. His gaze moved around the chaos as he heard various animals howl in unison.

Heather gasped.

"It's happening, Eric. Just like the first time. The beast is everywhere. In everything." More explosions punctuated her statement.

Eric nodded.

"Please, Rusty. I know what to do, at least how to put it back where it belongs. But we need your help. Please—we aren't strong enough to do this on our own."

Something in the neighborhood bully shifted. A life that had been without purpose, one that had once only taken meaning from the suffering in others, now found a reason to help someone.

"We're never going to be friends. Ever."

Eric and Heather nodded and in unison. "Fine."

Rusty turned his attention to his parents, now trying to make their way to their son. As he looked at them, he asked, "What do we do?"

Eric looked at Heather.

"We head to the barn. To its original cage."

"Then what?" Rusty asked.

"You two keep the possessed animals at bay."

Even Heather was taken aback. This was not what they had originally planned.

"Whoa, whoa, whoa, Eric. I thought we were going to just seal it off and Rusty and I were going to help cover it up after?"

THE TYRS IN REALITY

Eric nodded.

"Yeah, that was before the volcano went. Don't you see, the beast is loose again. There is only one way to fix this."

Heather started shaking her head. "No, no. No!"

"I have to go back into the Tyr. I have to lure the beast back in its cage."

Heather tried to talk him out of it, but it was Rusty that mustered the words.

"No backing out now, Stor—Heather. You pulled me in. We're doing this."

He looked at Eric. "I can't believe I'm saying this, but, lead on, freak."

And with that, the three most unlikely kids living in the outskirts of a twisted rural town in America went off to finish a story that started over a century ago.

22

FACING THE BEAST

The ash from the volcano had all but blackened the sky. Yet for all the terror Eric and his companions felt, there was also a sense of excitement. For his entire life, Eric had wanted adventure, a purpose beyond what life had dealt him. Here and now, with his only friend Heather and the most unlikely of allies Rusty at his side, the meaning was becoming reality.

Small fires were popping up all over Ashen Forest Estates. As they neared Eric's house, he could hear his mom and dad screaming for their son. Close by, fire engines and members of the volunteer fire department as well as the Grizzlydale police department were forcing people to leave their homes. Eric felt horrible as he saw two police officers hold his mom as they made her leave. She was yelling and screaming for her son, while her dad was doing his best to convince her that they were looking for Eric, that she would be no help right now. Heather saw the pain the scene was causing Eric.

"We can go to them. Just get the heck out of here. It's not

too late."

Eric stiffened.

"Yes, it is, Heather. We're the only ones that know the real danger. The fires. The quakes. That's all stuff the adults can deal with. But the Tyrs? That's us and us alone." Behind him, he heard Rusty mumble something about being grounded until graduation. Against his better judgment, Eric turned and smiled.

"You're assuming we live to see it."

Rusty shook his head and made an obscene gesture.

"Let's just get on with it."

Amidst all the chaos, Eric, Heather, and Rusty made their way to the barn. Horrible green energy spewed forth from under every crack and crevice of the barn. All around them, animals sensed their approach and started to charge. Normally the image of angry chipmunks and cats would be hilarious. But all the humor goes out the window when the animals begin shrieking in unearthly sounds and produce teeth that would dig into all but the hardest hide. Heather shook her head.

"That can't be happening."

The animals leapt at the three kids. Although he did his best to keep his cool, Eric let out a scream that pierced the disaster and caught his mother's ear.

"Eric!" she shouted. Breaking free of the unfortunate cops trying to help her, she made a beeline for the barn. "Eric! Franco! He's here. Franco! Help me. Eric is here!"

Heather and Rusty started swinging madly at the possessed creatures. Rusty let out a victorious cry as his bat connected with a small fuzzy creature. It was a nasty hit that should have left the poor animal little more than a mush of goo. Instead, the chipmunk let out a shriek as its broken body somehow mended itself with a sickly sound and pressed its attack. Both Heather and Rusty yelled extremely colorful phrases as they fought back. Then the three kids heard a cry that chilled them all as a massive dog burst from the barn and charged directly toward Earlina.

"Mom!" shouted Eric as the dog closed the distance. Heather began to cry in pain as she recognized her beloved pet Hoss as it made its way to her best friend's mother.

"No, Hoss! No, no, no!" She ran towards her twisted pet and Eric's mom, while Franco, along with other uniformed adults, ran into the danger.

It was then that Rusty addressed Eric.

"You do what you have to do. We'll take care of this!" Eric just froze as he imagined the horror that was about to unfold. Again, Rusty shoved him.

"Dang it! Now. Go!"

Eric shook off the terror and nodded. He took out the papers from the leather tube and ran straight into the barn. The entire time, he heard his mom crying out his name.

The ground shook again, the violence strong enough to uproot trees and cause older homes to collapse in on themselves. Eric pressed forward, pushed by an inner strength even he was surprised to muster, until he made his way inside the barn. Inside, the quickly breaking building was awash in bright green light from the largest open Tyr he had seen yet. He took a deep breath.

"Well, Eric. For better or worse, here we go." With a shout of defiance that he actually wished he'd given more thought,

Eric leapt into the mouth of the Tyr to face what was waiting for him beyond.

What he couldn't hear was his parents' shouts as their worst nightmare was made real as another quake shook the barn to its core, and the barn violently collapsed into a heap of smoldering rubble.

Inside the Tyr, the scene was strangely serene. The chaos seemed to only be happening on the other side of the opening.

"Tocho! Tocho, I need your help! The Tyrs are ripping open. Hairy Baby—ugh—Hemei Ninambebea is making its way into my world. My family"!

The quiet quickly ended as a roar cut through the bizarre forest. Eric snapped to attention with just enough time to leap out of the way as the most grotesque creature he could ever imagine leapt from the shadows. The creature slammed into a massive rock. A sickly cracking sound echoed in Eric's ears as what Eric assumed was the Hemei Ninambebea in full form fell to the ground. A horrendous slash down its back revealed the creature was no threat. Eric stood there, dumbfounded.

"Well, that was easier than I expected," he said aloud, as he approached the lifeless creature.

Slowly making his way to the beast, Eric began to wonder just what made this thing so dangerous, laughing to himself that his little tussle with Spit a few minutes earlier had felt more threatening. He pulled out the papers from the leather tube and looked over the writing and symbols. "Guess I won't be needing them after all." As he started to roll them back in the tube, a thought crossed his mind. In all the books he'd ever read, be they fantasy, science fiction, or the rare horror book, there was always one rule when it came to them all. Never be sure the monster is down. When you have the chance, finish it off.

"Yeah, that's probably a good idea," he again said to no one. Shifting through the papers, he tried to find the writing that put down the Hemei Ninambebea for good.

"That's weird. They all talk about containing, or holding; nothing about killing the dang thing." So lost was he in his own strange thoughts Eric did not notice the Hemei Ninambebea beginning to stir a few feet from him.

Back in Ashen Estates, a firefighter was doing his best to tend to the nasty wound Earlina had suffered as the hideously possessed dog, Hoss, tore into her arm. Although the bleeding had stopped, she was likely going to have a rather vicious looking scar, assuming they all survived the ordeal.

More and more possessed animals had begun to race toward the wrecked barn.

"I think they're trying to get to Eric. To build their own strength in their natural home," Heather guessed.

Rusty tried to comprehend what the lanky girl was talking about.

"So you mean we should be hitting anything that heads towards the barn?"

"Pretty much, yes. Ah!" Her words were cut short as a frighteningly thin cat leapt from under Eric's house and raked its fetid claws against her leg. She clutched at her leg with one hand, then spun wildly with her other and hit the demented feline square in the hind end, sending it flying against a tree. Just as had happened with so many of the other animals, whatever damage she might have caused only righted itself seconds later.

"There is no way we can hold out much longer. I hope whatever Eric has to do, he does it fast."

Rusty, ever the voice of support, replied.

"Sure. As if he's even still alive."

"You shut up!" It was the best Heather could offer, because part of her was starting to worry the neighborhood bully was right. Her negative thoughts were quickly replaced by survival as Hoss turned its attention on her and Rusty.

"Oh, no."

Back in the Tyr, Eric kept fumbling with the pages when from the darkness of the glowing woods, he heard a familiar shout.

"Stupid boy! What are you doing?"

Tocho's shout was cut off. Behind Eric, the Hemei Ninambebea let out a sickly roar as it righted itself and stood, a disgusting mass of broken legs and sinew. Eric stepped back in fear and the beast attempted to repair itself before Eric's eyes. Bones that once poked from under its rotting fur and skin slid back under and reformed. The sounds of muscle and tendons being repaired shook Eric to his core. It stopped and looked directly at him when it noticed the papers Eric was holding.

"No. Words. Magicks!"

Eric leaned forward against all better judgement.

"You can talk?"

Tocho raced with all speed to Eric.

"Stop speaking to it, stupid boy, it understands you. It understands everything"!? Run!" The reality of the moment finally popped into Eric's head. But not before the Hemei Ninambebea slammed a broken claw into Eric's shoulder and sent him flying back, toppling Tocho as she ran to him. Both of them let out cries of pain as they rolled harder against the ground. Eric felt himself losing his grip on the papers from Mr. Gregory—papers that had the words of power that would forever trap the Hemei Ninambebea. Papers that suddenly went flying to the winds.

"No. Words!" The Hemei Ninambebea stretched its body as bone and flesh mended itself. Through the pain, Eric saw the beast in its repaired form. It was the mountain lion from the beginning of The Tale of Tocho. Or at least, what had once been a mountain lion. The very predatory cat of which he'd first read when he opened the book written by the young woman that was trying to pull him back to his feet. He let out a shriek as the pain of the wound coursed through his body.

"This is so very bad. We don't have much time."

"Ah! God, I am so sorry. I didn't mean—"

"Stop. We must run. Now!"

Together, Eric and Tocho took off into the woods. The Hemei Ninambebea righted itself and gave chase.

"Heather! What is going on? Where is my son?" Franco was doing his best to maintain his composure, but she could see that he was only going to do so for so long. Behind her, Rusty let out a grunt as he batted away yet another possessed animal trying to make its way into the barn. A few had already gotten past him. The local bully was unaware of the power that was turning to the myth they all called Hairy Baby. That with each missed swing, the chances of Eric finding victory and even survival fell.

"I don't know, Mr. Del Bosque," Heather lied. "He said he needed to get his books."

Eric's father wasn't buying it.

"What are you talking about!? The whole place is crashing around us and you're telling me my son went to get books? From the neighbor's barn?"

Heather smacked another nasty critter from her back as Franco kicked a small dog aside.

"Young lady, you will tell me where my son is and you will do it now, and then we are getting out of here!"

Losing her focus on Hoss for just a moment to finally come clean with the adult, Heather never saw the oldest and most cherished pet in her whole young life barrel into her. She did, however, let out a horrible cry as Hoss's teeth locked onto her right arm.

"No! Heather. No!" was all Eric's Dad could muster as he reached out to her. She screamed more as Hoss dragged her into the green, gushing geyser that was once the prison of an legend made all too real.

Eric and Tocho ran as fast as Eric's wounded body would allow. No matter how fast they moved, the Hemei Ninambebea gained on them. Finally, Tocho slowed and lowered herself next to a large stump with a hollowed center.

"What are you doing?" asked Eric, clutching his bleeding shoulder.

"It has been a good hunt, Eric, but now we make our stand. Now we face the coming beast. And we shall face it standing tall."

Eric shook his head.

"No way. We keep running. We find a way to trap it forever. To send it back."

"If the mountain now burns in your time as well as mine, then the breaks in the land are complete. The end times, as spoken of by my Elders, is at hand."

Eric could hear the growl of the Hemei Ninambebea, slowing its pace as it drew near. He could swear he heard the beast taunting them both as it stalked them.

"So that's it. We just stand here and let it take us out?"

"Make no mistake, boy, we shall make it earn its kill."

"That's just stupid. No!"

Although Tocho looked scared, there was also a determination in her face. Her mind was at peace with what the beast offered her. Eric, however, was not ready to play out this ending of her story.

"Wait! I've got an idea."

They could both hear the Hemei Ninambebea get closer. Indeed, the silence of the green glowing forest was cut by a horrible laughter that shook them both to their core.

"Feast. Now," came the words from the Hemei Ninambebea.

Eric shook his head and mumbled to himself.

"I don't think so, kitty cat." He reached into his pocket. Blood was starting to drip down his hand. From his dirty and torn jeans, Eric pulled out a slip of plain paper. He smiled.

Tocho looked at him in confusion.

"You still have the spells?"

Eric shook his head.

"Nope, but I don't think he knows that." And with that, Eric stepped out from behind the large stump and stared the

Hemei Ninambebea dead in the eye.

"I call upon the powers of fire, sky, and earth! Send this beast back to the abyss!"

From behind him, Tocho whispered,

"What are you saying? Those aren't even the right words. Or the right language."

The ruse worked enough for the beast to take a step back. Eric felt a rush of pride as the beast actually cowered from his simple slip of paper. Eric pressed his advantage and began quoting every book he'd read and movie he'd watched. The Hemei Ninambebea backed away in fear.

"Yeah! That's right. Big bad Hairy Baby is afraid of paper! Wow! What a world ender you turned out to be!" Then, even shocking himself, Eric started to laugh. Tocho stood dumbfounded. The Hemei Ninambebea backed away more.

"See, now let's get the real spells."

Tocho shook her head.

"Boy, you do know it's been speaking in your tongue since you arrived. Yes?"

Eric turned back to the beast as it stopped backing away. Tocho continued her chiding of Eric. "And now it knows you lack the true spells."

He dropped the blank paper with more colorful phrase, followed by, "Run!"

They both did so, but it was of no use. Filled with rage at being duped, the Hemei Ninambebea charged at them with even greater power. Letting out a roar that rattled the trees, Tocho and Eric went tumbling to the ground. The Hemei Ninambebea did not pause in its attack and came at them with death in its eyes.

Behind them, the bright green shaft of light reached to the skies. Another massive Tyr opening, but where, Eric and Tocho had no clue. Then, Eric heard a cry that made him break inside. Heather Foster. His best friend was here, now, in the Tyr with the beast. The Hemei Ninambebea stopped its attack and turned toward Heather's cry.

"More. Energy."

Tocho and Eric got back to their feet and chased the Hemei Ninambebea as it went after Heather.

"Oh, no!" shouted Eric as he saw the horrible, altered Hoss standing over his bruised and bloody friend. She was still breathing, but Eric couldn't tell how bad off she was. The Hemei Ninambebea moved with a deliberate pace as the transformed Hoss stepped forward to its master. A sickly green energy began to spew from Heather's one-time companion and into the beast. Heather tried to get to her feet, but fell back to the ground in pain.

Tossing all caution to the wind, Tocho leapt into action and used her own body as a projectile against the Hemei Ninambebea. It stopped its energy drain of the dog, turning its attention back to Tocho and Eric. It swiped wide with its vicious claw and dug deep into Tocho. She let out a quick yell, but refused to go down.

"Eric! The real pages. Get them. Get them now!"

Eric ran from Tocho's quickly losing battle and grabbed the first pages he could find.

"How do I know which ones?"

"Just get them. Any of them!" Tocho gave a cry as the Hemei Ninambebea bit down and she fell to the ground. Eric screamed as the beast turned to face him and Heather. He looked at Tocho. She wasn't moving. Heather had gotten to her feet, an axe in her hand—the same axe Eric knew once belonged to the brave young woman now lying before them. He cleared his throat and, standing tall as the Hemei Ninambebea made his way to them, Eric began to read from the pages.

The Hemei Ninambebea charged. There was little distance between them. Heather raised the axe and threw it with all her might. Against all odds, the weapon found its target and buried itself deep into the body of the charging Hemei Ninambebea.

"Eat on that!" she yelled.

Eric, with grim determination, kept reading. All around them as he read, Tyrs began to shut and the beast quivered in pain. In a rare bit of good luck, the axe Heather had buried into the beast's body was not working its way back out. The wounds stopped closing all together as he read more from the page.

The Hemei Ninambebea made one last leap at them. Eric kept reading and Heather placed herself between the beast and her friend. The impact never came. Instead, both Eric and Heather heard the familiar growl of a dog.

Hoss, still disfigured from the effects of the Hemei Ninambebea on their world, jumped in and attacked the horrific beast.

As Eric read more, Heather screamed for her beloved pet.

"Hoss! No. Please. No! No! No!" Heather cried as the beast and her companion tumbled around. There was a quick howl and both stopped moving.

All around them Tyrs began to shut with violent energy,

each closure draining lifeforce from the Hemei Ninambebea.

It turned toward Eric and Heather.

"There isn't anymore to read. No more spells."

Without thinking, Eric gently reached out and took Heather's hand as one Tyr closed after another, the Hemei Ninambebea weakening bit by bit. Still, it drew closer.

Both friends closed their eyes. Even in its weakening state, it was more than a match for the two of them.

The Hemei Ninambebea grew closer still. Suddenly, its eyes widened and it turned away from them. Standing behind the beast, a horribly beaten Tocho grunted in pain as she again brought a large stone down on the beast. It spun and swung at her. She ducked. But even that motion was too much and Tocho fell to the ground.

She looked at Eric and Heather, knowing that she had little time left in either reality.

"Go. While you can. Go."

Eric shook his head. "No, no way. We beat this thing together."

Tocho smiled.

"That was never my destiny, Eric . Go."

More Tyrs closed. The beast slowed more, but still closed in on Tocho.

Heather pulled her friend with all the strength she could muster and together they both slipped into the last open Tyr before it sputtered and died.

They never heard Tocho cry out.

23
THE END OF SUMMER

Eric sat up in his bed. His arm still hurt from the events of early summer, but he was finally able to move it without wincing in pain. He slipped out of bed and looked out the window. The sun was bright and crisp. What was left of the burned and collapsed barn was gone, piled into the back of a large truck and hauled away weeks prior.

"Huh, looks like someone is buying the place." He made his way out to the kitchen. He still didn't understand why no one, save Heather and Rusty, remembered any of the events of early June. At least, not how they remembered it. The whole town rallied together when volcano bellowed for the first time in a hundred years and sent ash and smoke into the skies, which stayed dark for almost two weeks. Most of the damage caused by the quakes had been repaired. Old and faulty gas tanks, as well as historical homes, were repaired and brought into the modern era.

For all intents and purposes, Grizzlydale was back to its simple and boring old self.

"Simple, as if this town will ever really be simple."

Earlina's arm had also healed. A few days after he, Heather, and Rusty faced down Hemei Ninambebea-possessed animals, and very likely saved the town, he asked his mom how her bite was healing. Although she still had the scar, Earlina, along with every other adult at the scene of the crisis, said it was from flying debris caused by an exploding propane tank. Eric tried to argue with them at first, but considering he was already grounded for most of the summer for running off, he thought it best to simply drop the subject.

In fact, the little contact he was allowed with Heather, who had also been grounded, though not as long a time, reminded him of the words told to them by Mr. Gregory—that certain people in Grizzlydale were "Tyr-touched," and they alone could see and remember what the town really was.

Eric smiled as he sat at the kitchen table.

"You seem rather chipper this morning," said Eric's mom, handing him his first cup of coffee. Ever.

Eric eyed it.

"Seriously?"

She smiled.

"Sure, if you really want some. I think you're old enough."

Eric took a sip.

"Bleh."

Eric's mom let out a snarky laugh.

"That's what I thought." And she took the cup for herself. "Also, I spoke with your father last night. As long as you don't go wandering off, and I mean it, you can officially consider yourself ungrounded."

Eric's eyes lit up.

"Really?"

"Yes, really. It's been one heck of a summer. You can at least enjoy this last week. Also, I'm going to let you take all your books back. You've had enough outdoor adventures for a while."

They ate their breakfast in happy silence. As Eric got up and started to wash the dishes, he heard his best friend in the whole world outside talking to someone that sounded very familiar.

Eric leaned outside his front door and waved at Heather.

"I'm not grounded anymore!"

"Awesome!" Heather returned the wave and continued, "Hey, look at your new neighbor."

Heather turned aside. There stood Mrs. Fontana, a massive smile on her face.

"Good morning, Mr. Del Bosque. Your friend Heather here tells me you two had quite the summer."

Eric shot Heather a strange look. Heather smiled back as she rubbed the scar on her leg.

"Don't ask me how, but she knows. And she doesn't think we're crazy."

Eric asked his mom if he could go outside and see Heather and the new neighbor. His mom smiled and waved him off. With far more speed than his still-healing body should have allowed, Eric sprinted out the front door.

"Oh, Ms. Foster, I never said that much. Indeed, after hearing about what you and Mr. Del Bosque did, you are both quite mad."

Mrs. Fontana walked over to Eric and took his face in her hands. It was an action that would have caused the Eric of three months ago to back away. Today? Between Mr. Gregory holding his face and looking into his eyes, and now his old teacher this was something he was getting used to. Mrs. Fontana smiled again.

"I see Mr. Gregory was indeed correct. That is good to know."

Eric tilted his head.

"Good to know what?"

Mrs. Fontana only stood back up.

"Just good to know."

Eric shot a look at Heather, who merely shrugged.

"Wait, did you buy the house next door?"

"Of course. I've been keeping my eye on it for some time now." Mrs. Fontana shook Eric's hand, and patted Heather on the shoulder. "You're good kids. The town needs more kids like you two." She started to walk away, leaving the two confused friends to ponder what she meant. Then, she stopped in her tracks. Without turning, she reached into her handbag and pulled out a small stack of paper.

"I almost forgot to give you this." She turned and handed Eric the papers. He saw they were crudely stitched together into a very fragile book. Mrs. Fontana smiled, waved at Earlina through the window and made her way back to her new home, past the one-time lair of the great

Hairy Baby.

Heather scooted next to Eric.

"Well, what did she give you?"

Eric opened the pages. It was hard to read the handwritten text. But he clearly made out the names Tocho and Hemei Ninambebea. He flipped through some more. Doing what he'd never done in all his years as a reader, Eric skipped to the last page. It had a single sentence.

Welcome back to Grizzlydale, Eric Del Bosque. We missed you.

THE END

Aaron Duran is the author and creator of multiple graphic novel titles. This is his first foray into long-form fiction. He is a prolific podcaster, including Drive Time at the Drive In and the award-winning Geek in the City Radio. He currently writes for Newsarama.com while spending days in his not-so-rainy home of Portland, OR along with his fantastic wife Jenn, and his embarrassingly cowardly greyhound, Picard.